Smith's

MONTHLY

Every Month Original Novels, Stories, and Articles

USA Today Bestselling Writer
Dean Wesley Smith

TABLE OF CONTENTS

Smith's Monthly Issue #24

The Writings and Opinions of

Dean Wesley Smith

Introduction
TWO FULL YEARS

In late October of 2013, the first issue of *Smith's Monthly* came out.

Admittedly, this was a crazy idea, to put a full novel, serial novels, some non-fiction, and a bunch of short stories in a magazine issue, all written by me.

And do that every month.

Something like this magazine had never been done in publishing history. Not ever.

It hadn't even been tried before.

Occasionally, back in the old pulp days, one writer would fill an issue of one magazine or another, often with stories written under pen names.

And a few authors, Lester Dent to name one, wrote a novel a month for years.

But no one had tried filling a monthly magazine before every month.

Yes, I am that crazy.

Each issue over the last two years averaged around 70,000 words. Every month.

You are reading now the last issue of the second year.

Next month starts year three, and I will just keep doing this on into the future.

Why keep going?

Simple answer. Because I'm having a blast.

So there is one thing I want to be clear about here at the end of two years. Even with my ability to write and publish this many words every month, I would not have been able to keep this magazine alive and going without fantastic support.

The fine people at WMG Publishing Inc. have supported this project from the start. And the publisher, Allyson Longueira, has gone above and beyond the call of duty at times to help me stay on track.

Thanks, Allyson.

And Judy, the fantastic copyeditor who works there as well, has learned my

Thanks for the Support

Dean Wesley Smith

style and just helps me give you clean reading.

Thanks, Judy.

And my wife, the fantastic writer, Kristine Kathryn Rusch, has supported this magazine from the start as well.

When I suggested this idea the first time, she just laughed and said, "Well, if anyone can do it, it's you."

And then over the last two years, she has read novel after novel and story after story, sometimes on short deadline to help me stay on the monthly schedule.

Fantastic support. Thank you Kris. I could not have gotten to the end of this second year without you.

I couldn't even have gotten this started without your support.

But even with all the fantastic help at WMG Publishing and here at home, this project would have died a very quick death if not for the support of those of you who subscribed, taking a chance on a really crazy idea.

Thank you!

And for all the readers who buy the back issues. Thank you.

And thank you to those of you who support this magazine through Patreon and get the issues every month. There is a full page in the back of this issue thanking you all as well.

This idea of doing a magazine full of only my own fiction every month sounded crazy to start. But now, two years and 24 issues later, this magazine continues onward.

For me it has been wonderful fun.

I hope all of you have enjoyed reading the stories and novels as much as I have had writing them.

And I hope you will stick with me for more years into the future. I promise to keep you reading and enjoying stories and novels as best I can.

Thank you all.

—Dean Wesley Smith
September 20, 2015
Lincoln City, Oregon

Coming Next Issue in Smith's Monthly
STAR MIST
A Seeders Universe Novel

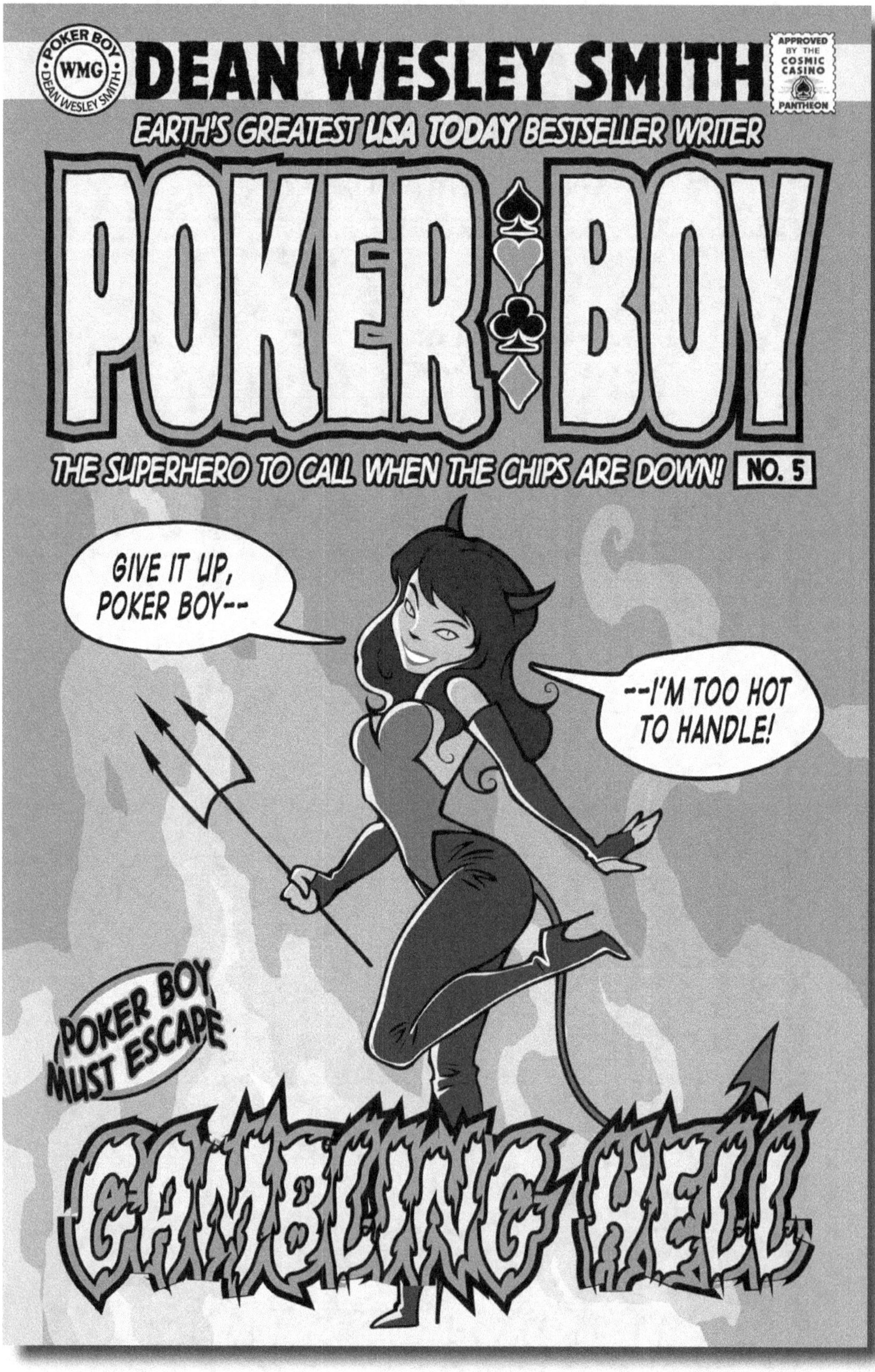

A beautiful woman sits down at a poker table and Poker Boy knows instantly everything feels wrong.

She seems beautiful, but her appearance hides something far more sinister.

Poker Boy, in a fair hand of cards, finds himself in a fight to save an entire table of innocent card players from ending up playing a very, very long and losing game in the poker room in hell.

First published as "Poker Boy vs. A Denizen of Gambling Hell" in All Hell Breaking Loose, *edited by Martin H. Greenberg from Daw Books.*

GAMBLING HELL
A Poker Boy Story

ONE

THE TEN-TWENTY HOLD'EM game at the Mirage was going just fine until Heidi sat down in the empty seat.

I was up about three hundred and enjoying the game, staying out of the way of another pro at the other end of the table. We were basically taking turns slowly relieving the tourists of their money, while making sure they had a good time giving it to us.

Heidi, with her long blonde hair, plunging V-neck sweater, and front-loaded assets shifted the feeling of the table. I sensed it at once, even without using my Ultra-Intuitive Super Power.

She gave everyone a bright, white smile, fumbled with her chips like she was a beginner, and then laughed at something the tourist beside her said that more than likely wasn't funny.

At once my Poker Boy Gut-Sense Power shouted at me like a voice coming up from the depths of the Grand Canyon. Normally the power never shouted at me unless I asked it to. Now the Gut-Sense Grand Canyon voice was echoing in my head.

She's a good player!

The breasts are fake!

She's evil!

As the superhero Poker Boy, I've fought my share of evil and played with more than my share of both good and bad poker players. The first because fighting evil is what superheroes do. It is the job description. The second because I make my living, pay the expenses to the next fight against evil, by playing professional poker.

Trust me, superheroes have to get money somewhere, and it might as well be from people who are enjoying themselves over a card game while they give me money to cover the costs of fighting those that needed to be fought.

Since the first day I put on my leather coat and Fedora-like hat that became my superhero costume, I knew that the Gambling Gods ran anything to do with gambling. Laverne, Lady Luck herself, was head of all things corporate, with Burt the General Manager running all casino operations in the god realm.

Stan was the main God of Poker and my direct boss. I liked Stan, and over the years I had actually met both Laverne and Burt during adventures. I knew them to be powerful and damned scary. No poker player I know of screws around with Lady Luck and lives to win another pot. I always treated Laverne with the respect she deserved and so far my luck had just been fine.

Of course, over the years there had always been evil to fight. Otherwise there would have been no need for my services as Poker Boy. But until Heidi sat down at my table, I had never faced evil over a game. And I had no real understanding that there was also a gambling hell where the evil I was fighting came from.

To be honest, I'm not sure why I hadn't put two and two together and come up with a gambling hell. The evil had to come from somewhere, didn't it? Besides, if there were Gambling Gods, I knew there had to be a gambling hell to keep the universe balanced. I just hadn't thought of it before I met the denizen of Gambling Hell named Heidi.

She had finished stacking her chips in a beginner-like manner, a neat triangle coming out from the rail, all chips stacked neatly in piles of five. Then she looked up at me and smiled.

Only there was nothing about that smile that reached her dark eyes.

I didn't move, didn't smile back, but it was clear from her look that she knew who I was.

And she was challenging me.

My Grand Canyon warning voice echoed in my head again.

EVIL!

Evil!

evil!

After the echo in my head died off, my next thought was to rack up my chips and just find another table, or maybe even call it a night. But I was a superhero, and superheroes didn't run from evil, they fought it, head on. Normally I had to go track it down, dig it out, and then vanquish it in some fashion or another. Evil had very seldom come to me and asked to be beaten like Heidi was doing.

But now Evil itself was sitting three chairs down the table from me in a ten-twenty game, directly across from the dealer, and I had no idea why. But I had a hunch I was about to find out.

The pro at the other end of the table, a man I respected for his great skill at poker and his ability to read just about any player, gave Heidi a quick once-over, shook his head, and racked up his chips. He knew, just as I did, that what had been a very good game had just gone sour.

"Good luck," he said to me before turning to leave.

I nodded at him and then glanced down at the two cards the dealer had just given me. Pocket kings.

I was two in front of the blinds so I raised the bet to twenty. Everyone at the table folded except Heidi, who pretended to fumble with her chips and had to have the dealer help her get her bet right.

She was good. Every man at the table was watching her, either her smooth-skinned hands or her plunging neckline.

The flop gave me another king, with two smaller cards that didn't match in suit or reach for a straight. Since I figured she was going to play the dumb blonde to the hilt and if I checked, she would check, I decided instead to bet ten more.

She again made a production out of calling. She was either giving me the first hand as part of the act, or she had aces and was playing me, pretending she didn't know what she was doing.

Then I realized there was something else going on. The calm, fun nature of the table was gone, replaced with tension and a focus that was distracted from the cards. It was almost as if the entire table had been shifted slightly out of the big Mirage Casino card room and into another dimension.

I glanced around. The rest of the room seemed distant and a little fuzzy.

So she wasn't just after the money, she was taking the table for another reason. As Poker Boy, I had seen a lot stranger things and for the moment I was willing to ride along to see exactly where we were going.

And why.

TWO

WITH THE TURN came another garbage card, with a rainbow, all four suits, on the board. I still had my three kings, but this time I just checked to her, wanting to see how she played her hand next. To a pro, in certain circumstances, a check means a weak hand. At other times it's a trap, meaning the hand is strong and the pro wants someone to bet so the pro can raise.

She looked at me with a puzzled smile on her face, pretending she didn't know what a check meant.

"Up to you," the young dealer said, resting his hand in front of the woman to indicate it was her turn to bet.

"Oh, it's my turn?" Heidi said, looking down at her cards again, then pretending to study the cards on the table. Then she looked up at the dealer, "What can I bet?"

A few men around the table who were taken in by her act chuckled. When a beginning player asked how much they could bet, it always meant they had a strong hand, or thought they had a strong hand. With Heidi I knew it was all an act.

But with that question, the room around us seemed to grow even more distant and blurry. The noise from the other tables faded farther into the background.

I had a sense of downward movement. No one else at the table noticed, including the dealer, as all their attention remained focused on Heidi, her blonde hair, and her V-neck sweater.

"The bet is twenty," the dealer said.

She fumbled with her chips and then slid twenty forward.

She smiled at the dealer and then looked my way.

I knew I was going to have to make my move pretty soon to stop what she was doing with this table, but I wanted to see that last card before I did. If she had two aces in her hand, there were still two aces left out, and I wanted to be sure that third ace didn't hit the board before I moved. So I simply flat-called her twenty.

The dealer patted the table to indicate the bets were all square, burnt a card and turned over the river card. A four of hearts that matched the four of clubs already on the board.

I had kings full of fours, the highest full house possible with the cards on the board. But not the highest hand possible. And that worried me a lot.

Around the table the rest of the Mirage poker room had become nothing more than a distant blur, the only sounds a faint rumbling. And the air was getting warmer and warmer by the moment. Heidi was moving the entire game into gambling hell, and no one but me seemed to be noticing.

I took a deep breath and focused on a spot between two upcoming seconds. I wanted to use what I had called my Unstuck-in-Time power. Stan the God of Poker had told me I had the power, and since then it had come in handy more than once.

My power froze everyone's movements except Heidi's. Clearly my power hadn't worked on her. She truly was evil and very powerful.

Seven of the men were frozen staring at her chest, the dealer and one of the other players were staring at her hands.

"Nice trick," she said, laughing in a way that made me shiver, even though I had on a leather jacket and the temperature around the table had gone up by twenty degrees.

By slipping myself between moments in time, I could see a little better where we were.

Granted, the Mirage poker room was a faint overlay, sort of blurred and fuzzy, but through that vision I could clearly see a huge cave with dark walls and bright lights hanging from the roof.

The table I was at seemed to be up near the roof of the cavern, still sitting in the Mirage, but yet at the same time floating in space, not yet all the way down to the surface.

A river of molten lava ran through one side of the cavern, accounting for the extra heat. There had to be at least a hundred different poker games going on around the room, all frozen because I was looking at them from a moment between seconds.

A poker room in gambling hell. This was the last place I wanted to be.

"So, Poker Boy," she said, smiling at me, "you hoping to freeze time and come and take a quick glance at what I have in my hand?"

I laughed at her. "Not my style. That's something you'd do I'm sure. I just wanted to stop this little elevator act you have going on."

"And you think this trick is going to stop it for long?" she asked, flaunting her chest assets by leaning forward and making sure her V-neck sweater bagged out just enough.

Granted, I was a man. But I had turned down sexual advances from a goddess far more interesting than her, so her attempts to distract me dropped short.

"Long enough to get this settled," I said.

"And just how do you plan to settle this?" she asked, smiling at me. "Knock me off my chair?"

I stared at her, looking deep into her eyes. In my years of doing superhero deeds, I had found many ways of solving problems, and none of them, not once, had I needed to use any physical-type action. Anyone who actually looked at me would know I wouldn't be any good at that stuff anyway. I kept my poker face on and just kept staring at her, trying to get any kind of read on what exactly what would work. Frighteningly enough, at the moment I didn't know. I was just playing a bluff.

THREE

SHE WAVED her arm around at the cavern. "You're in my world now."

I said nothing.

She shifted slightly, still smiling at me, still leaning forward trying to get me to look at her fake assets.

I just stared at her face, into her eyes, like I stared at any poker player who tried to make a move on me. And I made sure I kept us firmly planted between seconds of time.

After a long moment of me staring at her she shifted slightly again, then turned to stare back, her fake smile frozen on her face.

I could tell I was getting to her. But I still had no idea what to do to get this table and all the men around it back into the Mirage poker room. I needed some answers.

"So what do you want me for?" I asked. "Why these guys?"

"Customers," she said. "Got to keep the operation running."

"No winning allowed down there," I said, indicating the tables frozen below us in the cavern.

She smiled again, and for the first time the smile reached her dark eyes. "Never."

Right at that moment I knew I had her. Just like I did in any tournament before making an all-in bet, I went quickly back over what had gone on before.

She'd been pulling a scam on the first hand after sitting down, and had gotten impatient to take the table down into her own world. And I'm sure there was a reason she was impatient.

Then I realized why. If we had reached the floor of the cavern in hell, I'm sure I would have lost the hand we were playing. She would have been able to change her cards into pocket fours, giving her quad fours, the only cards that would beat my kings-full in this hand. That's why she was in a hurry to get the table down. She wasn't used to losing and she was going to lose the first hand.

But we hadn't reached the floor of the cavern yet. And I could still see the Mirage poker room outlined around us. That meant, I was sure, that real world rules played. That Laverne and Stan were still with me in spirit.

I leaned forward. "Any of these men actually due to arrive in your world today?"

She glanced around at the frozen faces staring at her chest. "No."

"So then you're basically after me. Right?"

She said nothing, but I could tell from her eyes that I was right. I also knew without a doubt I wasn't ever destined to go in this direction after I died. Besides, from what I understood, superheroes lived a long time, so I had no idea how long in the future any question about this issue was going to be.

"Why go after a superhero?" I asked.

She smiled. "Challenge."

"It must be getting dull in Gambling Hell."

She only shrugged and smiled.

I had played her right into my hand and there was no point in rubbing salt into a wound any more, even if the person was from Gambling Hell and didn't know they were even wounded yet. So instead I smiled at her for a few moments longer, just to get her squirming.

Then I said, "Well, if you like a challenge, how about we finish this hand to see which direction this table is going? I win the hand we go up, back to the Mirage and you go somewhere else to play. You win, we go down, and I'll go with you for a while. Play your game."

The moment I put it back on the cards I caught a slight, very slight hint of panic cross her face. She hid it well, but I still saw it. I knew I had her. She had a good hand, but she didn't have the nut hand.

"Well, let us go so the dealer can call the hand," she said.

"No," I said, not wanting this table to get any closer to that cavern floor. "Right here, right now. No more bets. We roll the cards and see who wins. Otherwise I call in Stan and he puts this table back where it belongs and you lose the chance of getting these players and me as your toys."

Heidi stared at me, taking her turn trying to read me. She was good, of that I had no doubt. But the best players in the world had tried to put reads on me for years without luck. No chance a simple Denizen from Gambling Hell could do it.

Finally she nodded. "You have a bet."

"I win," I said, making the bet clear, "the table goes back to the Mirage and you leave. You win, I release the table and we play in your world for a while."

"Those are the stakes," she said.

With that she flipped over pocket aces.

"Nice hand," I said.

And then I did something I never do in real life because it just annoys me and every other player. I hesitated in turning over my cards. It's called slow-rolling and it is the worst thing any player can do. But I did it anyway, just to get under Heidi's skin, just to give her a brief moment when she thought she had won. Sort of a little taste of her own hell is the way I figured it.

"Pocket kings," I said, flipping my cards onto the table face up in front of me. "Kings-full."

For a moment I thought I caught a glimpse of what Heidi really looked like under all that fake skin and large breasts. And let me tell you, she was one ugly human being. Nightmare ugly.

She stood, pushing her chair back and I let us go back to normal time at the same moment.

Suddenly the noise from the Mirage poker room pounded in around us. The men at the table were suddenly very surprised that Heidi was standing, and that our cards were showing without a final round of betting.

"Nice *playing* with you," she said, staring at me. Then without her false smile, she bent over and picked up her chips, giving a number of the men at the table a real show before turning and stamping off.

"What just happened there?" the dealer asked as he slid the pile of chips in the middle of the table toward me.

I shrugged. "Sore loser."

One of the men who had gotten the best show from her picking up her chips laughed. "She bends over like that a few more times and she can take all my money."

"Always be careful what you ask for," I said. "You never know where you might end up."

Everyone around the table laughed and the mood shifted back to a fun game of serious poker, playing for money instead of souls.

⌒

Now Available
from all your favorite booksellers in trade paper and electronic editions.

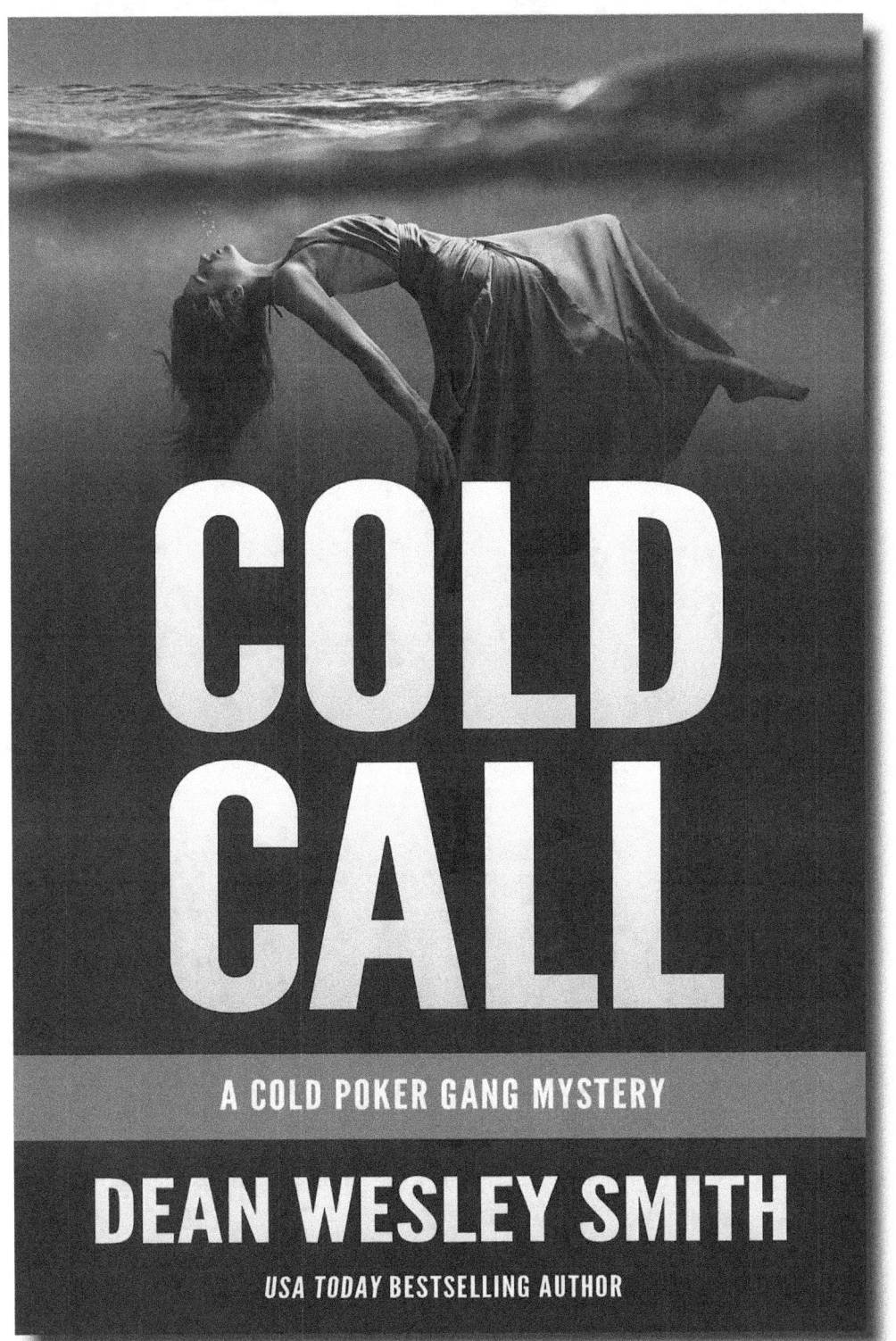

Dean Wesley **Smith**

USA Today Bestselling Writer

A
Twilight Zone
Story

Dead Post
Bumper

Elliot knew the world would not end in 2012.

But his wife thought it would, so on the morning of December 21st, 2012, Elliot went out for a drive to avoid her.

And found himself in the Twilight Zone.

"Dead Post Bumper" was first published in the More Stories from the Twilight Zone, *edited by Carol Serling and published by Tor in 2010.*

DEAD POST BUMPER

ONE

Elliot Leiferman: Summer 2016 near Death Valley

THE DUST AND LIGHT SAND swirled along the edge of the ancient road like a runner fleeing a threat, twisting in streamers on the dry desert wind, vanishing, then appearing a step or two later.

The sagebrush whipped back and forth making only a faint rustling sound quickly snapped away by the force of the hot wind and the empty nothingness of the desert. A fence of rusted wire and old wood paced along beside the road, sometimes upright, other times nothing more than a remnant of splinters mostly covered in sand.

The road, gray with age, vanished under sand drifts and piles of dry sagebrush as it stretched into the distance. Nothing but dust and sand and waves of heat had traveled the road in a very long time.

The rusting hulk of an old automobile rested on four flat tires, tipped slightly in a shallow ditch. One of its two doors hung open and the hood of the car was tucked against a still-upright fence post. The picture of a wildcat adorned the hood and the word Jaguar in metal script rusted on faded blue paint.

A man's body sat behind the steering wheel, the skin mummified in the heat and dry air and constant wind, the old seat belt still holding the body in position. Dead eyes stared at the fence post against the hood of the car as if it was an insult even to the living.

Dust swirled inside the car for a moment and then settled into the thick layer on the seats and floor.

Sand was building a dune against one side of the car, already up to the bottom of the windows. In ten more years the car and man inside would be nothing more than a large pile of sand and the highway would be covered completely.

TWO

Elliot Leiferman: December 20th, 2012, Malibu, California

ELLIOT WATCHED in disgust as his wife, Casandra Leiferman, Candy to her few remaining friends, grunted as she lowered her large bulk into a chair beside the bed. She had a chocolate-covered maple bar in one hand and a large vodka-tonic in the other, three limes of course, more vodka in the tumbler than tonic by a factor of two.

Nothing he could say, no amount of pleading, begging, threatening, had helped Candy to either stop her drinking problem or go on a diet. His thin bride of eighteen years had ballooned in just the last three years to over 350 pounds and she now regularly downed ten vodka-tonics in tumblers before dinner. He gave up counting how many she had every night after her huge dinner. She just passed out in her bedroom, eating and drinking while watching television.

He had moved into his own bedroom almost two years ago now.

Something had gone horribly wrong in both of their lives and their marriage, and he had no real idea what. He had remained thin, actually five pounds under their marriage weight, and he seldom drank anymore. His work took him around the world on business trips and for years Candy went with him on many of the trips.

But then, three years ago, it all changed and changed suddenly. She started drinking and eating and quickly grew tired of the traveling as well, deciding instead to simply stay at home and indulge herself.

At one point, a year ago, he had begged her to go to counseling with him and she had shrugged and gone along. But in the sessions it quickly became clear she was never going to stop either overeating or drinking. She just didn't seem to see why she should.

When the counselor finally got her to tell him why, clearly, so that she, the counselor, could understand her, she had simply said, "Why not."

"I *still* don't understand," the counselor had said.

Candy had looked at her with disgust, then said simply, "You haven't heard? The world is ending December 21st, 2012. So why shouldn't I enjoy this last year?"

Since that point, Elliot and Candy had argued many, many times over her belief. He had kept asking her what if she was wrong, what then? She had flatly said time and time again that she wasn't wrong.

He had demanded over and over for her to explain how could she be so certain.

The Mayan calendar is ending on that date," she had said, as if that explained everything. "I just know my life, your life, will end that day. I can feel it."

Now, as he unpacked from his last trip, she sat in his bedroom on his dressing chair.

"Tomorrow's the big day," Candy said between bites of the maple bar and sips of the vodka-tonic. A large smear of chocolate streaked her cheek but she didn't seem to care. She hadn't been out of her bathrobe in weeks and he doubted from her sour smell that she had even taken a shower in that amount of time either. He had been in Europe the last two weeks and had only gotten home a few hours before.

"So," Elliot asked, repeating a question he had asked every time she said something about her insanity, "what happens if the world doesn't end tomorrow?"

"Oh, it will," she said before taking a huge bite of the maple bar, chewing twice, then washing it down with a large gulp of vodka.

Elliot just shook his head. How could a woman he had loved so deeply, still loved, actually, gone so far off track? He had read a dozen books about insanity and nothing about Candy seemed to even fit a pattern. He could even remember the night it had started. Back in 2009 she had come to bed late after watching a History Channel special on how the world was supposed to end on December 21st, 2012, the last day of the Mayan calendar. She was both excited and agitated at the idea, and he had listened only half-heartedly at what she had said that night.

Over the next few weeks after that, she never stopped talking about the topic, even on a trip together to London, one of her favorite cities. At one point on that trip she stood looking up at Big Ben and said, "Isn't it a shame that all of this will be gone in three years?"

He had changed the subject, hating even talking about predictions of any future. That was for those crazies who believed in that mumbo-jumbo. He was a believer in right now. The present. Today. The future would be what the future would be. And Candy, up until that point, had been as down-to-earth as he was.

Not any more. She was as crazy as they came.

He turned from his unpacking and looked at the mess of a human being his wife had become. "I guess tomorrow we shall see, won't we?"

"That we will," she said, smiling. "I plan on spending the day on the deck, watching the world end over the ocean. Would you like to join me?"

"Thank you, dear," he said, turning back to his now almost empty suitcase on the bed so that she wouldn't notice how disgusted at her he felt. "I'll do my best to make it back from the office in time."

"With the world ending, why bother to go into the office at all?"

He shrugged, keeping his back to her. "I just like the routine is all. It's comforting."

"Well do hurry home," she said. Then grunting, she hefted herself out of the chair and waddled down the hall toward the kitchen.

He had no intention of being home tomorrow, end of the world or not. He'd deal with her the following day, after her fixation had been proven wrong.

Then maybe he could help her, find her the help she needed.

THREE

Elliot Leiferman: December 21st, 2012, near Death Valley

THE CAR HIT NINETY easily as he took the Jaguar down the straightaway out onto the desert road headed toward Death Valley. The old highway was almost never used anymore, and to even get on it he had had to move a road-closed sign, but he loved the freedom of the straight pavement and the speed he could safely drive without worrying about any patrols stopping him.

Thunderclouds threatened in the low hills in the distance, but the cab of the Jaguar kept him comfortable from the intense heat and safe from the blowing sand. This morning Candy had been like a schoolgirl in her excitement. How anyone could be excited about the end of the world was beyond him, but for weeks the news reports had gone on and on about the Mayan Calendar coming to an end today, and this morning's headlines were "End of the World?"

The entire thing just annoyed him.

It was not only stupid, but it had cost him the woman he loved. He wanted this past, he wanted to help Candy get healthy again, stop drinking, lose weight, become the woman he had married.

But that wasn't going to happen until he got home tonight and the world hadn't ended. Then he could start helping her recover for real and maybe even get to the root cause of why she had believed the end was coming anyway.

The smooth ride of the Jaguar ate up mile after mile of the old road, taking him deeper and deeper into the desert.

Even at this time of the year, the temperature outside his car was a warm ninety degrees and he had the air conditioning holding him in comfort. He had come to learn that there were real advantages to having large amounts of money, the beautiful home in Malibu was one, this car was another.

He loved this car, and lately had taken more and more long drives in it when home just to get away from Candy.

He looked out over the expanse of desert around him, letting himself relax into the drive. Wouldn't it be funny if the world actually did end today while he was in the desert? He snorted to himself and snapped on the radio, letting it search for a radio station.

Normal music playing, no alarms, nothing different.

Nothing was ending today.

He let the miles drift by as he thought about all the wonderful times he and Candy used to have and the hope that starting tomorrow, they could rebuild that old life once again.

The sun was starting to touch the horizon; the day was nearing an end. Candy was going to need him later tonight. He had no doubt she would pass out from all the drinking, but at least he could be there to take care of her. For the first time in a year, he felt he wanted to. Something that she had believed in deeply was about to not happen and she would need help getting through that.

He let the car slow down to under sixty and glanced around at the vast expanse of nothingness. Amazing that in such a crowded place as California, there could be so many thousands of square miles of nothingness.

At that moment he noticed a faint light on the dashboard. He slammed on the brakes and came to a stop in the middle of the old road.

The gas warning light was on.

Oh, God, no. He had no idea how long it had been on, but it was unlikely he had enough gas to make it back to the roadblock he had moved, gone around, and then replaced. That had to be seventy or more miles back at least.

It had never occurred to him to get gas before he left. His thoughts had been on Candy and the end of the world, not his wonderful car.

He swung the Jaguar into a quick three-point turn on the narrow old road, and started back west into the glowing orange of the sun as it set over the Pacific in the far distance.

He had to stay calm, think this through.

At that moment the finely tuned car that had run so smoothly for so long sputtered, caught again, then sputtered and shut down.

He was out of gas.

On a closed old highway near Death Valley.

Oh, God, oh God, oh God, what had he done?

The steering was heavy in his hands as he took the car out of drive and coasted to a stop.

At the last moment he eased the car off to the side of the road, letting the Jaguar come to rest in a very shallow ditch, its front bumper resting lightly against an old wooden post of a long gone fence. No point in taking a chance that someone else out speeding on this old road would plow into his car in the middle of the night. He just hoped that bumping the old fence post hadn't scratched the bumper.

He snapped out his cell phone and looked at the signal.

Nothing.

And he had never bothered to have a tracking satellite system installed, even though the dealer had suggested it. He had never figured it would be needed in his drives around Malibu.

He glanced around.

Death Valley.

A closed road with no traffic.

Nothing within seventy or more miles from him.

God, oh God. What could he do? His stomach twisted like he was about to be sick.

He couldn't let himself panic. He had to think this through. If he panicked, he was as good as dead.

He pushed open the door and let the hot wind of the early evening blow dust into his just cleaned car. In front of him, the sun had set.

He glanced at the clock on the dashboard. 5:30.

Six-and-one half more hours for the world to survive to prove he was right and Candy and all the other doomsday shouters wrong.

He unbuckled his seat belt and climbed out of the car, standing in the middle of the road in the fading light and looking in both directions, fighting down the panic that threatened to choke him at any moment. His only hope of getting out of this stupid mess was to stay calm.

No point in trying anything until light. Even with the sun just barely set, he could feel a bite to the air. It was going to be a long, cold night.

He went back to the Jaguar and checked for anything that might help him make it more comfortably. Nothing. He kept the Jaguar's truck clean enough to eat out of, and he had not thought to bring either food or drink with him.

He had on light slacks, a light shirt, and not much else.

He went back to the car, buckled himself back into the driver's seat, reclined the seat just slightly, and shut the door.

He had no idea just how cold it got later that evening. But it was colder than he had ever experienced or imagined possible.

FOUR

Elliot Leiferman: December 22nd, 2012, near Death Valley

THE COLD HAD DRAINED Elliot more than he had ever imagined it could. His stomach was threatening to claw its way out of his body from hunger, and his lips were already chapped from no water and the extreme dry air.

At sunrise, he had managed to stagger out of the car and back onto the road. Then he had started walking back toward the roadblock at the same pace he used on the gym's treadmill, a steady 4 miles per hour.

After an hour his speed had slowed and he knew, without a doubt, that he had no chance of making that walk clear back to the roadblock. The intense cold of the night was already being replaced by the hot, dry heat of the day, and the constant wind and blowing sand seemed to suck every ounce of moisture from his body.

His only hope was to return to the car and pray that someone either spotted him from the air or happened to drive by. Even if Candy noticed he was missing and reported that to the police, no one would know where to look. He had never told anyone he used this old highway to take drives on.

He barely made it back to the car, again snapping himself into his seat with his seat belt and leaving the door open for ventilation.

Yesterday clearly hadn't been the end of the world, at least not for Candy. But it might have been for him unless he got very, very lucky.

That night, after a long, very hot day, the night again got bitingly cold and thunderstorms echoed through the desert, sending flashes of bright white light to show him the vast wasteland and how hopeless his situation really was.

A flash flood also washed out the bridge near the roadblock that night, making it impossible for any car to travel the old county road again.

The next morning he again started off on the walk out, but this time turned around after just a mile, almost too weak at that point to make it back to the car.

He slept off and on through the rest of the heat of the day and into the biting cold of the night, his seat belt holding him in place. The hood of his car and that fence post learning against the bumper of his Jaguar became his entire world as he drifted in and out of consciousness.

By the third day, Elliot's strength was gone. He could barely keep his eyes open as the intense heat of the day drained away what will to live he had.

His mind escaped the constant of the old fence post, drifting back to the good days with Candy, the fun they had had, the trips they had taken.

Candy had been right.

If he had just listened to her, drank with her, ate with her, got fat with her, enjoyed the last three years as she had done, he wouldn't be sitting where he was, dying from the heat and thirst and hunger, staring at on old fence post.

He had caused the world, as he and Candy knew it, to end on the last day of the Mayan calendar.

He had caused it by not believing it could happen.

Yet it had. The world had ended.

"I'm so sorry, Candy," he managed to whisper through cracked, dry lips.

As he slipped off into his last sleep, the sun beating down on the top of his Jaguar, he asked one last question, hoping somehow that Candy could hear him all the way out in Malibu.

How did the Mayans know?

USA TODAY BESTSELLING AUTHOR

DEAN WESLEY SMITH

AN EASY SHOT

A GOLF THRILLER

In the first installments, Seattle Police Detectives Bonnie and Craig, while taking a late night walk on a Scottsdale Arizona golf course happen to overhear a conversation between two men plotting to kill a United States Senator.

At the same time, a young golf professional's wife is kidnapped. Scheduled to play with the Senator, he must do what they ask or his wife will die.

Bonnie and Craig get the FBI and local police involved. Everything is set and they play with the Senator to help protect him.

Nothing goes wrong, but that night, they again see the two men who they had overheard.

Now, the next morning, starting the second round of golf, everyone waits and watches.

A horrific accident on the golf course almost kills the Senator, but he is fine and sent on to Washington while they set a trap for the man coming to kill Danny, the young golf professional.

The man is killed in the hotel room by Craig and an FBI agent.

Danny's wife is rescued and at that point Bonnie and Craig think they can now go back to their vacation. Nope.

AN EASY SHOT

Part 7 of 8

CHAPTER TWENTY

Monday, April 10th
1:06 a.m.

CHARLES ROBINS SAT back in his chair and smiled as Grant reported the security measures being taken around the estate.

Charles figured that if he was going to have a problem with the man he called Bill because of the short payment, it was going to be tonight.

Or maybe tomorrow night.

So he had called in every member of his security team, under the leadership of Grant, an ex-Marine who knew more about defense and killing than Charles ever wanted to know.

He had told Grant who he needed kept out and Grant had said it would be no problem.

His people would keep everyone out.

Charles was just fine with that.

Grant had just finished explaining the basic defenses of the estate. He had two dozen men, all with state-of-the-art weapons patrolling both the grounds and the house. Three men watched the security monitors at all times, taking shifts. Automatic alarms had been set on every inch of the grounds' parameter. Grant was convinced that nothing was coming in that they didn't know about.

"Only one problem I see, Mr. Robins," Grant said.

"What's that?" Robins asked. The last thing he needed tonight was problems. So far everything had gone perfectly. Senator Knight wouldn't be voting later in the day and that was just about as perfect as it got.

"An FBI surveillance van is parked across the street from the main gate," Grant said without moving his hands from the parade rest position he had been standing in for five minutes, "and they have three other men stationed around the parameter of the estate in observation locations."

"FBI?" Robins asked, his stomach suddenly twisting in fear. "Are you sure?"

"Yes, sir," Grant said, "I'm sure. You pay me to be sure."

"Any idea why they are out there?" Robins asked.

"No, sir."

"Are they making any move to come in?" Robins asked.

Grant shook his head. "No, sir. They are strictly in surveillance mode."

Robins nodded. "So anyone coming in here would have to get past them as well as your people."

"No one will get past my people," Grant said. "But the FBI, in the configuration they are working out of, would make no move to stop anyone. The fight would be ours, sir."

Robins nodded. "Thank you, Grant. I will talk to you in the early morning."

"Have a good evening, sir," Grant said. He spun and moved briskly out of the study, the heels of his boots making no sound on the hardwood floor.

FBI? What were they doing out there?

He felt himself panic and he forced himself to take a few deep breaths, his palms flat on the hard wood of his desk top.

Clearly someone had put the vote tomorrow, and the implications to his companies' future, together with the Senator's accident. And since the FBI had failed in keeping the Senator from having his little spill down the hill, it would make sense they would cover all bases.

He forced himself to take more deep breaths and relax and think.

If anyone could prove anything, or even had a shred of evidence besides speculation, the FBI would have come in and taken him. So the fact that they were just in observation mode was good news as well.

That thought released his fear.

Of course. They had nothing on him but motive. And motive wasn't enough to move against someone like him, even if they did prove it wasn't an accident.

Charles stood and moved over to his bar and poured himself a small glass of his finest scotch. It was almost time to get some sleep. The legislation that would have killed his companies would not be passed. And by the time it could come up again, he would have enough votes controlled to stop it completely.

He had won.

He should learn to relax a little and savor the victories.

He downed the Scotch and moved toward the back entrance of his study that led up to his bedroom.

A few hours sleep was exactly what he needed.

CHAPTER TWENTY-ONE

Monday, April 10th
1:37 a.m.

BONNIE KNEW THAT even with Craig's plans of sex tonight and tomorrow morning—which she liked the sound of a lot—they were going to be lucky to stay awake long enough to make it happen. The last two days had been very stressful to both of them, and after the dip in the soothing warm water of the hot tub, Craig looked almost as tired as she felt.

Yet she wanted to make love to him as much as he said he wanted to make love to her. She could feel the desire slowly building, but she wasn't going to push it to happen tonight. They still had tomorrow and tomorrow night. More than enough time before heading home. She was just happy that they were out of the entire mess with the Senator.

She brushed her teeth and crawled into the wonderful-feeling clean sheets, letting them soothe her almost as much as the hot water had done earlier.

Craig had just finished brushing his teeth and was coming out of the bathroom naked when there was a knock on the door.

He glanced at her and she shrugged. One-thirty in the morning wasn't a normal time for anyone to come knocking.

"Who is it? Craig shouted at the door, moving at it to check through the peephole.

"Room service," Bonnie heard a man's voice on the other side respond.

Craig looked through the hole in the door, then said, "We didn't order any room service."

"Yes, I know, sir," Bonnie heard. "This is from a friend. A surprise."

Something was bothering her about that voice. About all this, but she couldn't put her finger on it.

Craig glanced back at Bonnie and just shook his head. Then he shouted through the door. "Hold on a second."

"Who would send us something at this time of the night?" Bonnie asked Craig as he climbed into a pair of shorts and padded back toward the door.

"I'm betting on Hagar," Craig said. "Or the Senator."

Bonnie nodded. That was possible. The Senator was a kind-enough man to do something like this all the way from Washington D.C..

But still, there was something wrong here.

Craig opened the door and stood back as a man in a hotel uniform pushed a food cart into the room.

"Hello," the man said to Bonnie as she held the sheets up under her chin.

Bonnie felt a shock run through her. She knew that voice from...

Suddenly, just as Craig was about to let the door close, two other men burst in, both pointing pistols at Craig.

"What the...?" Craig said, backing away from the door with his hands raised.

Before Bonnie could even react, the man in the hotel uniform pulled out a pistol and leveled it at her, motioning for her to remain still.

She pulled the sheet up even farther over her breasts and stared at the man.

The guy just smiled in return.

The door closed behind the three armed gunmen with a resounding thud and Bonnie suddenly knew that she and Craig were far from out of this entire mess. In fact, they had just become part of the mess.

"I would suggest you both put some clothes on," the man in the hotel uniform said. "You're going for a ride to visit a friend." He smiled. "I told you it was a surprise."

Now Bonnie absolutely knew the voice. She would remember that voice anywhere. Standing in a hotel uniform with a gun pointed at her was the second man they had overheard on the golf course on Friday night.

She glanced at Craig, but he was staring at the two guns pointed at him.

"Let's go, people," the man said. "We honestly don't have all night."

Bonnie hadn't let another man see her nude since she married Craig, but at the moment it looked as if she didn't have much choice in the matter. She had no doubt this guy would shoot her without a second thought. And dying in this hotel room wasn't in her plans for the future.

She tossed the sheet aside and stood, moving over to where she had dropped her shorts and blouse when she had put on her swimming suit. With her back to the man, she dressed quickly.

By the time she turned around to again face the guns, Craig had on a golf shirt and was slipping on tennis shoes.

She retrieved her tennis shoes from near the bed and put them on as well.

When she stood, the man in the hotel uniform said, "Good. Now all three of us are going to walk down the hall and through the hotel lobby to a waiting limousine I have out front."

He pulled off the hotel uniform jacket and untucked his shirt to make himself look like a guest.

Craig glanced at Bonnie, but said nothing.

The man pointed his gun at Craig. "Detective, one false move in the hall or lobby and your pretty wife here will be the first to die, I promise you. My men and I have no problem firing in a public place. Chances are she will not be the only person to die. Am I understood?"

"Perfectly," Craig said.

"Good," the man said. He indicated they should go.

One of the gunmen opened the door and took up a position out in the hall, his gun inside a jacket pocket, but still very much in evidence.

Bonnie moved through the door beside Craig and walked beside him down the hall with the men following.

The ride down the elevator was long and uncomfortable, since Bonnie and Craig stood facing the door, the three men behind them. Bonnie could just imagine the three guns pointing at the small of her back. She didn't like the feeling at all.

The walk through the hotel lobby was just plain frightening. There had to be twenty people standing around or walking through the lobby. Couldn't they see what was happening?

It seemed that no one did.

There were no shouts or alarms and a few moments later they were out the front door, down the steps, and into the back of a waiting stretch limo.

The three men sat facing Bonnie and Craig. Two had their guns in their hands. The man clearly in charge just sat back and smiled.

Bonnie didn't feel like smiling back.

"Relax and enjoy the ride," the man said. "We don't have that far to go."

Neither Craig nor Bonnie said a word.

Bonnie had no idea why they were being taken and any question she might ask would only chance giving the man information he might not have. So she said nothing.

Outside the streets of Scottsdale flashed past, the night traffic very light on this early Monday morning.

CHAPTER TWENTY-TWO

Monday, April 10th
1:49 a.m.

CRAIG TRIED TO make sure he knew where they were, where they had turned, and what part of Scottsdale they were in. He wished he was more familiar with the area, but if needed, he might be able to retrace the steps from the hotel to the general area they were in now.

Maybe.

Their kidnappers sure seemed unconcerned that he was able to see where they were going. And that lack of concern bothered him. It usually meant that the kidnappers had no thoughts of ever letting them go.

The limo finally pulled over beside an open area, just short of a massive stone wall that towered twenty feet over the street and stretched for a least a half mile.

Craig could see that there were a number of very large estates nearby, the biggest more than likely behind the wall. But right at this spot there was nothing but empty desert.

"Okay," the man said. "Time for a little talk."

He motioned for the two other gunmen to get out of the limo and then close the doors. When they did, he turned back to face Craig, smiling, his gun in his hand leveled on Bonnie's midsection.

"Just listen," the man said. "I have no desire to kill either of you. But make no mistake, I will if I have to."

Craig nodded and out of the corner of his eye he saw Bonnie do the same.

"First off, my name is not important. Charles Robins calls me Bill, so we'll just go with that."

Craig started at the name of Charles Robins. What was this guy up to anyway?

"I'll tell you this right up front," the man said, "Charles Robins hired me to stage an accident with Senator Knight so that Knight would not be able to vote later today in Washington on a piece of legislation that would hurt Robins."

Craig desperately wanted to tell this guy that he had failed, but knew that wouldn't be a good idea at this point. The guy would find out soon enough as it was.

The bigger question is why this guy was telling them all this information?

"I have put tapes of my conversations with Mr. Robins in a locker at the train station." The man flipped Bonnie the key.

She was so surprised that she almost didn't catch it.

"The locker number is on the key. If you get out of this alive, that's the key to the locker."

Craig, in all his years of police work, had never been this confused before. "So why are you telling us this?" Craig asked.

The guy laughed. "I suppose this all does seem a little odd to a police detective used to criminals trying to cover their guilt instead of admit it."

"A little," Craig said, as sarcastically as he could.

The man snickered. "Trust me, Detective, I will never be caught for this crime."

Now Craig understood. "But you want Charles Robins to be, is that it?"

"Exactly," the man said.

"Why?" Bonnie asked.

"Because the man wouldn't pay me what we agreed he should pay me for the work I did."

Now it was Craig's turn to laugh. "The old saying comes back to bite you, huh?"

The guy smiled at Craig. "You are right, detective. No honor among thieves is how the saying goes. But I keep my word and I expect others to do the same. Charles Robins did not."

"And now he must pay the price," Bonnie said. "Is that it?"

"Exactly," the man said.

"So couldn't you have just called the police, left the tape, and ran like hell," Craig asked. "Why go through all the problems of kidnapping us?"

"For one I would have never had the pleasure of seeing your fine wife here without clothes on."

Beside him Craig could feel Bonnie tighten even more, but she said nothing and didn't move.

"Secondly," the man said, going on, "Charles Robins is an idiot and I want to make sure he is so deep into this mess that no amount of money will buy his way out."

"And that's where we come in," Craig said. "Right?"

"Exactly," the man said. "Let's go."

With that he opened the door, and with the point of his gun, indicated that they should get out of the limo.

Craig climbed out with Bonnie behind him, followed by the man.

Outside a third man had joined the other two. He was very large and muscled, with a military posture and build. He was perfectly proportioned and as Craig got closer he realized the guy had to be at least six-four.

The big man nodded to the one who had been talking to them in the limo, then turned to the other two guards. "Tie their hands behind their backs."

Each guard did as he was told.

Craig could feel the rope being pulled painfully tight as he attempted to keep his wrists apart and his muscles flexed.

"Ow!" Bonnie said, glancing back at the guy behind her. "Not so damned tight. I might need those hands again."

After they were finished being tied, the tall man turned to the guards. "Take our two prisoners to Mr. Robins' study, then have him awakened. Give him this note."

The big man handed the guard behind Craig a piece of paper.

"Through the front gate, sir?" the guard asked.

"Does it matter to you?" the large man demanded, moving up into the guard's face. "Or would you like me to do it and find someone to take your place?"

The big man towered over both Craig and the guard.

Craig could hear the guard swallow behind him.

"No, sir," the guard said, clearly afraid of the big man.

Smart thinking.

Craig wouldn't want to tangle with the guy either.

"Now follow orders," the big man said. "I have another task to complete."

The guard pushed Craig down the street while the other shoved Bonnie ahead of him.

After about twenty steps Craig glanced back over his shoulder. The man they had overheard on the fairway on Friday, the man who had told them he was hired to complete the plot against the Senator, was climbing back into the limo with the larger man. Both were laughing.

That made Craig shiver.

Craig looked ahead at the distant front gate to what must be Charles Robins' walled estate. And just to the right, sitting peacefully on the street, was the white van Craig knew held the FBI observers. Maxwell was going to go nuts when he saw this on tape.

If Craig had had his hands free, he would have waved as they passed.

And that was exactly what the guy who had kidnapped them had wanted.

He and Bonnie were bait.

The FBI was the weapon.

And the target was Charles Robins.

Craig had a feeling that getting him and Bonnie out of this alive was going to take more luck than he wanted to admit.

CHAPTER TWENTY-THREE

Monday, April 10th
2:17 a.m.

CHARLES ROBINS DIDN'T much like getting awakened in the middle of his sleep. And tonight was no exception.

Yet the guard didn't seem to want to let it go.

"I'm sorry, sir," the guard said, his voice seeming to blare over the private intercom. "It is important that you come to your study at once."

"I'll be right there," Robins said. He crawled out of bed slowly, rubbing his face. Screw going right there. He was in charge here, and he'd get down there in his own damned time.

It took him ten minutes to put on clothes, use the bathroom, and pour himself a glass of juice before he finally went down the private stairs to his office.

He expected Grant to be there with some problem, standing at attention in front of his desk like he always did. But instead he saw two guards with a tied up man and woman. Both the man and the woman were in shorts.

"What's this all about?" he demanded.

"Charles Robins, I presume," the tied man said.

"And just who the hell are you?" Robins asked.

"I'm Detective Frakes," the guy said, smiling. He nodded at the woman beside him. "This is Officer Stanley. We're both with the Seattle police department."

Robins felt his stomach clamp up into a tight ball. These were the two who had been playing with Senator Knight all weekend. What in the hell were they doing here?

"What were you two trying to do, break in to my estate?"

The man shook his head no. "I'm afraid your men came and got us from our hotel room bed."

Charles glared at the guard. "Is that true?"

"Yes, sir," the guard said.

Charles just stared at the guard, not really believing what he had been told. His men had kidnapped two cops, the same two who had been playing for two days with Senator Knight, from their hotel room and brought them to his study.

"Why would you do that?" Charles almost screamed. "Where's Grant?"

Charles stared at one guard, then the other.

The guard behind the tied-up detective stepped forward. "Grant told me to give you this note, sir,"

"Note?" Charles asked. "I don't want any note. I want to talk to him. Now!"

The guard only shook and looked afraid, so Robins took the note and opened it.

Dear Charles,
Since you saw fit to short me one-half-million dollars for the job you hired me to do on Senator Knight, I felt you deserved something for my troubles.
Enjoy,
Bill

Underneath the first note there was a second hand-scrawled note in another color pen. It said:

Dear Mr. Robins,
I cannot work for a man who would hurt a Senator and kidnap fellow police officers. I quit.
Sincerely,
Grant

"Damn, damn, damn," Charles said, reading the notes over again. There was no chance at all of being able to show this note to anyone. He stopped and looked up at the guard. "You said Grant gave you this note?"

"Yes, sir," the guard said.

"Was there another man with Grant when he gave it to you?"

"Yes, sir," the guard said. "A man who called himself Bill."

Suddenly the past few years were all making sense. It was no wonder this Bill person could get into the estate through the security so easily every time he was called. He and Grant, his chief of security, had been working together all this time.

And now the guy had made Charles look as if he had ordered the kidnapping of these two police officers. And that might be enough to tie him to what happened to Senator Knight. With the motive, it was more than enough, that was for sure.

Charles moved over and sat down behind his desk, trying to clear his mind.

He had to figure out what to do next.

And no option looked good.

"Sir?" the guard asked, "what do I do with the prisoners?"

Charles glanced at the two cops, then shook his head. "Put them in a closet and guard them until I decide what to do next."

"But sir," the guard said, "the FBI knows they are in here."

"Of course they do," Charles said. "Don't you think I know that? Now do as I say. And for god's sake, don't hurt them."

As the two were being led out Charles drank his juice as calmly as he could. He hadn't thought of the FBI. The man named Bill had set a perfect trap.

Charles leaned back and looked around at his beautiful study. With the Senator not voting tomorrow, he was going to keep control of his fortune. And that meant he could afford the expensive attorneys who could get him off this hook.

He would blame Grant and the man named Bill as getting greedy, as taking too much control in his problems. His lawyers would get him off as a man who let his employees take too much control.

He could feel the plan starting to form. In a few hours he would turn over the two detectives personally, claiming he just had learned about the plan.

If he worked it right, with enough spin and good enough attorneys, he might just come out of this all right.

CHAPTER TWENTY-FOUR

Monday, April 10th
2:36 a.m.

THE GUARDS SHOVED them both into a small hall closet and closed the door, plunging them into darkness.

Bonnie bumped against Craig and then used the right wall of the closet to get her balance. The ropes around her wrists had become painful about ten minutes after they had been put on, and now they were just a dull ache. From what she saw before they were shoved inside, the closet had a few coats hanging in it, all on wooden hangers. Nothing more.

"You all right?" Craig whispered.

"Fine," she whispered back, keeping her voice soft enough so that no one outside the closet could hear. "Just completely confused."

She still couldn't believe what had happened to them.

Taken from their hotel room by a man who wanted to frame another man. Then told about it.

It was just too weird.

"Seems like we're pawns in a game between murderers," Craig said, his voice low and coming out of the darkness. "I sure don't much like that idea."

"I couldn't agree more," she said. "That Charles Robins gives me the creeps."

"Slime describes him just fine," Craig said.

"So what do you think is going to happen next?" Bonnie asked. "You think the FBI guys saw us?"

"They would have had to be asleep to miss us," Craig said.

"It's getting lighter in here," Bonnie said.

Her eyes were adjusting to the dim light coming through under the door and around the cracks in the casing. She could barely see the outline of Craig leaning against the other wall a foot or so from her.

"It is," Craig said. "And we have to be ready for anything that's going to happen next. How tight are your ropes?"

"Tight," she said. "But I can still move my fingers."

"So can I," he said. "You want to try untying mine first?"

"Sure," she said, turning her back to him. "Let me get into a stable position and you put your ropes in my hands."

"Good idea," he said.

Bonnie leaned forward, head against the wall for balance. Behind her she could feel Craig's hands against hers. Then he lowered his hands so that her fingers were on the ropes around his wrists.

The knots felt tight and it took her a moment to find a place to even try to start working the knot loose.

Then she noticed that Craig's fingers were between her legs, against her crotch because of how she was leaning forward.

She moved her butt slightly. "This could be more fun than I thought."

He laughed lightly and moved his fingers against the seam of her shorts, keeping his wrists still so she could work on the knot.

She could feel that she was making a little progress, but not much. "Can you move your wrists to your right slightly, and turn them to the left?"

"Sure," he said. As he moved to the right he slipped one finger under the leg of her shorts and pulled up as he twisted his wrists to the left.

That put two of his fingers right up against her bare flesh. She made herself focus on untying the knot.

"No underwear," he whispered. "Nice."

His fingers moved back and forth.

She tried to focus on the knot, and it seemed to be coming free slowly, but Craig's fingers were distracting her.

"That feels wonderful," she said softly. "But you're not helping me get you untied."

His fingers stopped. She desperately wanted to push back against them, but the fear of losing the progress she made on the knot stopped her.

She forced herself to work at the rope, ignoring the sense of his touch against her crotch.

What seemed like an eternity later she said, "I think I've almost got it."

His fingers slid a little farther along her crotch.

"I'd agree with that," he said, the humor clear in his voice even in the dark.

"You keep that up and I'm never going to get this untied," she said.

"Nothing but promises," he said, laughing as his fingers moved a little again and then stopped. The movement sent chills through her, and small ripples of pleasure swirling in her stomach.

She focused on the knot, finally pulling it free.

"Got it," she said.

"Nice job," he said. "Stay put and I'll untie you."

She could feel his hands working on the ropes on her wrists, and as he did she moved her butt back against his crotch.

"Now you're the one slowing down this process," he said.

"Well then hurry up and get me untied," she said, moving her butt slowly back and forth. She loved teasing him, just as he loved teasing her.

Finally she felt the wonderful relief of the ropes coming off. She stood up and rubbed her wrists, trying to get circulation back through them. She had no doubt she was going to have bruises there for weeks.

"Now what?" she asked.

Craig kissed her quickly, then turned and pulled one of the wooden hangers off the bar. He slapped it against his hand. "Get one and let's see if we can get out of here."

She did as he suggested, the weight of the hanger in her hands not giving her any reassurance at all.

Craig turned and carefully tried the door handle. It was locked and as he tried to turn it, the knob rattled.

"You two stay quiet in there," a guards voice came from the other side of the door, loud and very, very close. "You'll be let out soon enough."

"Shit," Craig whispered.

Bonnie turned and put the hanger back on the hook, then sat down on the floor, her back against the back wall of the closet. They weren't getting out of this closet any time soon.

She watched as Craig gave the closet one more close inspection and then sat down beside her.

"What a way to spend a vacation," she whispered.

"As long as it's with you," Craig said, "I'd spend it locked in a closet."

"We are locked in a closet," she said.

"Oh," was all he said.

To be continued…

Dean Wesley Smith

*USA **Today** Bestselling Writer*

Cheerleader Revelation

Sometimes to save the world,
a guy must take on the cheerleaders.

Sometimes, to save the world, a guy must take on the cheerleaders.

John Divine lived through a vision of the end of the world, a world ruled by cheerleaders, a world he refused to live in.

His choice obvious.... He must stop them.

CHEERLEADER REVELATION

ONE

JOHN DIVINE, leader of the chess club, scholarship student next year to MIT, and total geek, hated cheerleaders. To him they were vain, shallow, stupid, and mean-spirited. They ran in packs like wolves, preying on any unsuspecting geek stupid enough to be in their path in the hall between periods at Jericho High.

Because he didn't look like the average geek, but instead was tall with thick shoulders like his father, he had managed to avoid contact. But that didn't reduce his hate for them.

Trudi Stevens was their leader, the worst of the worst with her long blonde hair, bright white teeth, and perfect body. He often had nightmares about that body, waking up sweating and shaking with a raging hard-on. After every dream about her, he was disgusted at himself.

It didn't stop the dreams.

Then one night in October, John had a dream like no other.

It was as if a spirit had come to him in his sleep, talked to him, given him a vision of the world to come, the worst vision of ruin that John could have ever imagined. People screaming and running nude in the streets, others being helped out in clear pain, others just standing mute in shock.

It felt like the end of the world.

And all in vivid color.

In the vision, he kept thinking over and over how real it felt, that he never dreamed in color, that he didn't want to even think about the end of the world. He was going to MIT next year. The world couldn't end yet.

As John fought to get out of the vision, it slowly changed, fast-forwarded in an odd way, showing him that humanity was gone from around him.

Except Trudi.

She stood there, towering over him, surveying the ruin and tragedy around her as if she liked what she saw. She was naked, hands on her hips, nipples hard and thrusting forward.

Cold wind blew her blonde hair and she didn't seem to notice. Only the ruin seemed to please her.

Then John realized he was below her, looking up at her, seeing how she shaved her crotch, how her butt stood out a little more than he had ever noticed before, how she had a dimple on one side of one ass cheek.

All in color of course.

Then she looked down at him and smiled that damn perfect smile of hers. As she did the sky cleared, the sun came out, and everything around him suddenly cleared.

She took a deep breath that did amazing things to her chest, then motioned that he should join her on the hill, climb up to her naked body.

Right then he woke up screaming.

Or maybe shouting.

TWO

"YOU ALL RIGHT?" his dad hollered down the hall from the living room. His dad had been unemployed for six months while his mom worked at a bank. She got up early and left for work, his dad stayed up late and watched old movies.

John was their only child and just sort of stayed out of the way. He had long ago figured out that the only reason they were still together was that he hadn't gotten out of high school and left yet.

"I'm fine," he shouted back. "Just a nightmare."

His dad didn't answer, which was normal at this point.

John left his bedroom as soon as his erection was down enough to not be noticed through his pajama bottoms, and went to the bathroom down the hall in the three bedroom home. His body was shaking every step of the way as he tried desperately to get the dream out of his head.

Get the image of naked Trudi out of his mind.

Only it hadn't been a dream. He was sure of that. It had been a vision, and no matter how hard he tried, he couldn't shake the fact that what he had seen was different.

That it was real.

It was the future.

By the time he had gotten his drink of water, peed, and gone back to his room, he knew for a fact that Trudi would cause the end of the world. He was sure of that, as sure as he was about the answer to the last question on a physics test. He just didn't know how she would end the world.

Yet.

So beginning the second month of his senior year at Jericho High, John Divine set out to stop her in any way he could and save the world from all cheerleaders like her.

As with any good scientist, he knew he first had to study the problem, meaning Trudi, before finding the solution. Since any science geek in high school was basically invisible to the popular groups, he easily followed her, tracking her schedule around school.

He knew when she was in English, when she went to cheerleading practice, and what her new Volkswagen with a red flower on the door looked like. He had it all written carefully down in notebooks, just as he did his lab experiments, noting every detail because you never knew when one would matter.

Then, with his dad's camera, he took a dozen pictures of her at different places around the school and put those in the notebook as well.

But after a month it was clear to John that nothing in his preliminary study had given him any ideas on how to stop Trudi from ending everything.

Or even any idea how she might do it.

Maybe she would become a power-hungry President of the country in thirty years. She had become class president after all. Maybe she would cause a war by saying something stupid at the wrong time in the wrong place. He just didn't have any idea, yet the vision of her standing there naked haunted him every day.

He needed to take his study of her to the next level. He needed to know what she did after school, in the morning before school, and on weekends. For all he knew she was part of an alien advance force coming to take over the planet.

Granted that had been done to death in movies, but that didn't make it any less possible.

He had to find out.

But taking his research to the next step posed a number of problems, not the least of which were the anti-stalking laws.

Finally he came up with a solution. From an online security sight he bought a very expensive miniature surveillance camera with short-range broadcast capability. It took a nice chunk out of his college bank account using the debit card for the purchase, but he figured that saving the world was worth it.

He boosted the camera's range to over a third of a mile and hid it on the underside of her rearview mirror in her car.

She couldn't see it. But the beauty of his positioning of the camera was that it would tell him where she was going, as well as showing her from the waist down if she were in the car. That way if someone else drove her car, he would know it.

He set up two relays, one near her house and the other near the school, to send the signal from the camera to the computer in his bedroom where he could record it.

The first three days of the new system she climbed in her car, left school, and just went home, climbing out of the car there and not using it again.

But on Friday afternoon, after cheerleader practice, he was already home and at his computer watching the feed live when she climbed into her car in the school parking lot and sat there for a minute, turned sideways as if talking to someone.

Then she did something that he knew for a fact he was going to have even more nightmares about. She raised her butt off her seat, reached under her cheerleading uniform, and pulled off her uniform pants and then her white underwear.

The vision had been right. She was so vain she shaved everywhere.

And he had an instant erection.

THREE

A MAN'S HAND and arm came across the field of vision of the camera and dove into her crotch like a mouse going for cheese after finishing a maze.

Her legs went apart and the hand played a piano solo on her key parts.

John watched as the hand moved, slowly gaining speed.

Then through the front window John saw two of the other cheerleaders come from the football field area and start toward the parking lot. It took Trudi and the extra hand a few moments longer before they saw the problem.

The hand yanked back as if scalded by a hot iron, and Trudi quickly slipped on her cheerleader pants, leaving her panties under the seat.

John had no doubt that the mouse would have a return match with the cheese after the game, but he didn't plan on watching.

Suddenly John realized he had the answer to stopping her. Those panties, tucked back under the seat, were how he could stop her.

In one of his experiments in class, and after class, he had been working on a possible chemical that would break down the molecular structure of synthetic fiber. If he could get that to work, maybe he could figure out a way to embarrass Trudi so much she would never be able to rise

to a position of power enough to destroy the world.

In a few minutes Trudi drove her car home, and then thirty minutes later drove it back to school for the big game, never getting her white panties from under the seat.

The moment she parked her car in the school lot and got out, John headed for the front room to ask his dad if he could borrow the car for a few minutes. He told his dad he needed it to go back to school for a homework assignment he had left there.

"Figures," his dad said, shaking his head while downing a beer. "Friday night and you're doing homework."

"A kid as good-looking as you are should get out of the books once in a while," his mother said.

"I know," John said, ignoring the conversation that had gone on for years now.

"Dinner's in forty minutes," his mother said, handing him the keys.

"I won't be that long," John said, and dashed for the car.

Twenty minutes later he was home with Trudi's underwear stuffed in his pocket.

The next Monday he was back in the chemistry lab doing experiments on a tiny patch of cloth cut from near the seat area of the panties.

Things after that settled into a routine for a few months. He studied her movements, watched the hand grab for cheese a number of times, and worked in the lab. As far as his professor was concerned, he was working on a way to make the molecular bonds in clothing stronger, to make clothes last longer. His professor followed his progress closely, astounded that he could do the work he was doing.

It was in January, on a late evening session in the lab, that he finally hit on the chemical compound he had been looking for. It was colorless, and easily contained by glass.

The beauty of his find was that when one diluted drop was put against a piece of the cloth, nothing happened.

But when a certain frequency of sound was directed at the treated cloth, the cloth broke apart and completely vanished in less than thirty seconds.

John could barely contain himself he was so excited. Even his mom noticed at dinner and asked him why he was so happy suddenly. He'd told her a good grade in a tough class and she nodded and patted him on the shoulder. His dad had only shaken his head.

John knew he was a disappointment to his father. His dad had wanted a jock, a football player with a mouse hand. Instead he'd gotten a geek kid with a computer and a desire to save the world. Maybe someday John would make him proud.

Or at least make him rich.

FOUR

FOR THE NEXT two weeks John repeated his experiment in private, making sure it actually worked the way he wanted it to. His teacher thought he was still stuck and hadn't made a breakthrough. John figured there was no point in having any way to trace what was going to happen to Trudi back to him.

After that he worked on his plan to really embarrass her, and end all chance of her causing the end of the world.

First he studied Trudi's home, thinking he might get his "Cloth Away" as he was calling it, into her laundry room, but soon tossed that idea out. Her parents were security freaks and her mom was always home. No chance of getting his new chemical in there.

So instead he studied the city's water supply and discovered that it would be easy to get his harmless, tasteless, odorless chemical into it. Even with the higher security these days, only one old guard sat in a truck near the fenced off lake. John could come down out of the trees on the other side of the lake, duck under the fence and simply put his chemical into the water.

He spent a week doing the calculations on how much he would need, then another week making the ten gallons of Cloth Away.

Then he studied the city's water supply, calculating how long it would take for the water with Cloth Away in it to get through the system and to Trudi's home. Then adding three extra days to give her time to do some laundry, he figured out the exact night and went up to the inlet area of the supply from the lake and casually dumped his stuff into the water.

Seven days later, much to the pleasant surprise of his father, he went to a basketball game, making sure to wear only clothing that hadn't been washed in the last few days.

He sat just off to the edge of the student section, and got there early enough that he was only one seat off the floor level.

Trudi and the other cheerleaders led the students in a few yells as they arrived, but mostly just huddled off to one side and talked and laughed, sometimes staring at the basketball players.

John tried not to stare at her, tried not to let the vision of the end of the world fade from his thoughts.

Around him the stands had filled. They were playing a team from sixty miles away, and most of the fans across the court were from there. That was good, because the frequency of sound he needed to make Trudi's uniform drop away would be hard to exactly control.

Finally, John could wait no longer. Trudi had been bouncing up and down along the sidelines during every timeout, and as the coach again called one, the cheerleaders took the court.

John eased the battery-powered horn out of his pocket, and with a deep breath, clicked it on, sending the silent ultrasonic sound across the court at the bouncing cheerleaders.

At the woman who would end the world.

Suddenly it became clear that he had miscalculated a little with the intensity of the sound from the horn.

The cheerleaders uniforms all sort of crumbled, dropped to the floor, and vanished, leaving the stunned girls screaming and covering themselves.

Around him John heard others shouting and screaming as the ultra-sonic sound from his horn bounced off the walls of the gym and came back and hit everyone in the home team stands.

Amazing how many people had done laundry in the last few days.

John instantly turned off the horn and hid it in his jacket, but the damage was done.

The very overweight woman sitting beside him lost her dress and underwear. Just about everyone in the stands around and behind him found themselves suddenly and completely nude.

People of all ages and sizes.

It was not a pretty sight.

Panic set in as people shouted and screamed and tried to cover themselves and run for the doors at the same time.

The visiting team and fans just stared in shock as even the home team basketball uniforms vanished.

John was pushed hard from behind and tumbled head-over-heels onto the gym floor, banging his elbow and head. He just lay there, on his back, eyes closed, trying not to think about what he had done.

A couple people accidentally kicked him with their bare feet in the stampede for the doors.

He never opened his eyes. It would have been too painful to watch the damage. It hadn't been Trudi that had ended the world, it had been him and his horn.

Finally the screaming and panic were over, ending almost as quickly as it had come, leaving only a low level of talking and uncomfortable laughing of the visiting team.

He finally got the courage to open his eyes.

People were still moving in all directions and Trudi was standing over him, completely nude and not seeming to care.

It was the same image as in his vision.

Around them the game, the world of high school Friday night basketball had ended

And just like in his vision, there she stood.

She bent down and extended him a hand to help him to his feet. "You all right, John?"

"I think-think so," he said, stunned that she knew his name.

"Good," she said, nodding. "You took a nasty fall there."

He rubbed the back of his head and laughed. "Yeah, I did. But I'll live."

Then he realized he was talking to Trudi, the woman he hated, the woman who he had thought was going to end the world in his vision. And she was nude, just as his vision had said she would be.

He quickly slipped off his coat and helped her put it on. The coat was long enough to cover just about everything.

"No point in getting too cold," he said.

She laughed as around them dozens and dozens of the remaining nude people who hadn't stampeded into the cold winter night were slowly getting covered back up by helpful people.

"Thanks," she said, zipping up the coat to make sure everything stayed covered. Then she felt the large horn and battery pack in the front pocket of the coat.

"What's this?' she asked, squeezing the hard horn from the outside of the coat and winking at him. "You happy to see me or something?"

"Always," he said, smiling at her.

"I know," she said, "considering you followed me around school for a month and then put a camera in my car."

In all his life John had never been so surprised, so shocked. How could she have known? He glanced around the basketball court where a hundred people still milled trying to figure out what to do next.

All he wanted was to run and run hard, maybe leave town. Maybe leave the country.

Why hadn't she reported him? Did she know that he had watched her and the football player's mouse hand? He could feel his face turning red.

"How did I know?" she asked, laughing at what must have been a shocked look on his face. "You're not the only one who's going to MIT next year, you know."

Now he was *really* shocked.

Trudi at MIT? She was a cheerleader. He hadn't heard she had gotten into MIT. He hadn't even given it a thought. How closed minded had he been?

The answer to that question was easy: *Very.*

"What I want to know," she said, holding onto his arm clearly to make sure he didn't run, "is how you managed all this?"

"Chemical breakdown of molecules," he said, "triggered by sound."

She patted the horn in the pocket of the coat she was wearing. "Brilliant. And you put the chemical into the city water supply, right?"

He nodded.

"Brilliant again," she said.

Then she laughed the most beautiful laugh he had ever heard. "Don't worry, your secret is safe with me. I haven't had this much fun in a long, long time."

"Thanks," he said, looking into her blue eyes and realizing that there really was a depth in there, a person with a real brain and a real sense of humor. "But to be honest it worked a little better than I had hoped."

"Only aiming at the cheerleaders, huh?"

She looked at him, smiling.

"Of course," he said, his tension of her knowing what he had done easing. "Actually, you more than the others?"

"Wanted to embarrass me, huh?"

"That, and see you naked," he said, finally admitting to himself the real drive behind his idea, planted by his vision.

"Well?"

"Well what?" he asked.

"Well what did you think of me naked?"

"Perfect," he said, smiling at her. "Worth every minute of the end of the world."

"Seems to me the world is just beginning," she said, smiling up at him. "How about you walk me to my car and drive me home to get some clothes? Then over a pizza that you're going to buy me I want to hear every detail of this crazy idea."

"And then?" he asked, smiling at her.

"Then," she said, taking his arm and turning him toward the gym door, "if you're a really good boy, I'll let you blow your horn again."

"I like that idea a lot," he said, smiling back at her.

The end of the world had never sounded so good.

~

Now Available
from all your favorite booksellers
in trade paper and electronic editions.

USA TODAY BESTSELLING AUTHOR

DEAN WESLEY SMITH

THE HIGH EDGE

A SEEDERS UNIVERSE NOVEL

Dean Wesley Smith

USA Today **Bestselling Writer**

For Your Consideration

A BRYANT STREET STORY

Sometimes, what we all wish for can happen in the Twilight Zone.

Other times, our wishes come true on just a simple suburban street.

Caro Rosefield must investigate a very strange foreclosed home. A nightmare or maybe a new future?

On Bryant Street, anything seems possible. And anything can happen.

FOR YOUR CONSIDERATION
A Bryant Street Story

ONE

CARO ROSEFIELD parked his rented Chevy Suburban near the curb of the quiet suburban street in a newer subdivision on the edge of the urban sprawl of Boise, Idaho. He left the engine running to keep the air-conditioning on since the temperature outside had just gone past one hundred and he didn't do well with heat. It made him light-headed and often sick.

The forecast for the Boise Valley was even hotter tomorrow. He hated July in general and he really hated it here in city plopped between a desert and a mountain.

He had his suit jacket in the back seat, his briefcase on the passenger floor, and the foreclosure paperwork for the house he was parked in front of on the seat beside him. Usually he never did anything without that jacket on, but it was just too hot to wear.

A couple of his friends teased him that since he had finished college he was never seen out of a suit. And dressing down for him was taking off the jacket. Caro had laughed at the ribbing, but it had hit home.

He didn't used to be like this. He liked backwoods biking and playing softball. But he'd been so busy lately, he couldn't even drag his six foot frame out to see his oldest daughter play softball. He kept his hair short now, but in college it had been long, and now he was even getting a pot gut from sitting so much, something he hated but couldn't seem to find the time to do anything about.

He had three homes in this city his employer, Secured Construction and Management, wanted him to deal with. They had bought hundreds of foreclosed homes around the west. And were buying more every day for next to nothing and then flipping them. They were making money off the misery of families who had lost everything.

His job was to get the foreclosed homes in shape to sell. He was what they called "Shoes on the ground."

After he got these three homes here worked around, he could be back on the plane and out of this heat, back to his home in Portland, Oregon, where the normal color was green instead of dried brown.

He hated being away from his home and his family so much, especially his two daughters. They were getting to that age where things were changing every day, and if he blinked twice, they would be grown and gone and he will have missed them growing up completely.

He hated that the most about this job, but in these times, any job was a good job. Someone had to pay the mortgage and buy the clothes.

He checked the address on the paperwork one more time, then studied the split-level home that was his assignment at the moment. Nice home, about four thousand square feet, two levels, three bathrooms, large lot, two-car garage.

But this house looked to be a problem. A huge problem in fact. In three years of getting repossessed houses ready to show for sale for his company, he had never seen anything like what he was seeing now.

The house was already perfect.

In fact, the first time he had spotted the address, he figured he was on the wrong street.

But he wasn't. The house was 2761 Bryant Street.

He was on Bryant Street. Right town, right state, right legal description, everything. And the house had 2761 in clear numbers on the siding near the front door.

He picked up the stack of white papers and checked the address one more time.

Yup. That was the exact address on the papers that said this house used to belong to a couple named Davis who had lost it to First Trust Equity a year ago. First Trust Equity had then gone out of business and sold the house to his company four months ago. He had been put on the job to get the house ready to sell. He was to hire a team of local contractors and cleaners, get it into shape, clear out any signs of the previous owners who had lost the home, and then get the property listed with a local reality company.

But this house was clearly not empty as it was supposed to be.

The lawn had been freshly mowed and a paint truck was parked in the driveway. A paint crew of three men was actively working on a new coat of tan paint.

He had heard of people squatting in empty, bank-owned properties before, but never painting them. Something was very, very wrong here and he had a hunch he wasn't going to figure it out quickly.

In fact, more than likely this problem might be something for the lawyers to untangle.

Someone, somewhere, had screwed up and he was about to tell that fact to the fine people in this well-kept home that they clearly cared for.

Damn he didn't want to do that. He wasn't supposed to deal with people other than painters and cleaners and real estate agents. Never owners or squatters.

He had heard of things like this, just never been a part of it before.

He wished on this hot July afternoon, he wasn't a part of it now.

TWO

HE GLANCED DOWN the road. Four homes had sale signs in yards and all four seemed empty, lawns not watered or cut, and one empty house two doors down the street had a garage door that looked like it needed replaced. None of those homes were his concern. At least this trip. The way housing prices were dropping in this city, he had no doubt he would be back.

He hoped that next trip it wouldn't be so damned hot.

The house two doors up the street was the kind of place he expected to find here at 2761 Bryant Street. Not a well-kept two-story being freshly painted.

He leaned back into the blowing stream of air-conditioning and studied the place. Clearly the water was on since the lawn was a lush green and the power was turned on as well, since one of the painters had a compressor plugged in and working.

Water and power companies did not do that for squatters, only home owners who could actually prove ownership.

"Oh, damn," he said to himself. "What a mess."

He let the cool air blow over him for another moment, then said, "Better get this over with."

He shut off the car and decided to just leave his jacket in the back seat. He even left the paperwork on the seat and just took his company business card with him. He had a hunch this wouldn't go well and he would be on the phone in a few minutes letting the company lawyers sort it all out.

He climbed out into the hot afternoon air. The heat wrapped around him like a choking rope that made his throat dry and his skin feel like it was flaking off.

His sweat didn't even last on his forehead it was so dry and hot.

How could anyone live in this kind of heat?

He headed for the front door, feeling like he was in a modern *Twilight Zone* episode. He had spent a lot of nights in hotel rooms watching old episodes of that show.

He could almost imagine Rod Serling standing off to one side of the freshly-mowed yard, smoking a cigarette, looking at the camera, saying, "For your consideration, one Mr. Caro Rosefield, hard worker, by-the-numbers kind of man, now faced with a dilemma pitting a corporation against a family's home. Mr. Caro Rosefield, the first shot of a war that can be seen being waged every day, not in the *Twilight Zone,* but on every street in every city just like this one."

Caro shook his head. The heat was getting to him. He hoped like hell Rod Serling wasn't standing over there talking like that. This situation was strange enough as it was.

He rang the bell as the guy with the paint gun moved around to the far side of the house. How was it even possible to paint in heat like this?

A young, smiling woman answered the door and a man in a golf shirt and blue slacks appeared a moment later behind her.

She looked to be thirty and had on a blue summer dress that accented her clearly athletic body. Her long blonde hair was pulled back and tied and she had a smile that lit up the area around her.

Her husband looked more like a golf professional than anything else, with a short-sleeved Izod shirt and blue slacks. He had close-cropped brown hair and also a smile on his face.

Both had good tans and looked like models out of a sports magazine.

"Yes?" she said.

Caro stuck out his hand and gave his full name, then handed them his business card.

"Come on in out of the heat and the paint fumes," she said and held the door open for him.

He stepped inside and was hit with a shift in temperature of at least thirty degrees. It felt heavenly and made him break out into an instant sweat.

"Thank you," he said, sighing as she closed the door behind him. "I'm from Oregon. Just not used to this heat."

The entryway showed a clean home with a living room of modern and expensive furniture, all tastefully organized. Through the windows, Caro could see the back yard was as well taken care of as the front.

These people had clearly lived here for a long time. A very long time.

The husband stuck out his hand. "Ben Davis. This is my wife, Stephanie. What can we do for you, Mr. Rosefield?"

Suddenly Caro knew what was happening. Ben and Stephanie Davis had been the names on the property before First Equity foreclosed. More than likely these fine people had been paying their mortgage all along and the payments had gone into some scam or another.

This was worse than he thought. These people were about to have one of the worst days of their entire life. And he was the one who had to deliver the message.

"I'm afraid I don't know how to even approach this," Caro said.

"It's about the house, isn't it?" Stephanie said, smiling, not looking worried in the slightest. "Come on into the kitchen and we'll talk and I'll get us some lemonade."

Caro nodded, feeling even more puzzled then he had before. Maybe Rod Serling really had been standing out there on the driveway.

"I'd love that," he said and followed them into the kitchen that looked like it had been remodeled recently with new granite counters and state-of-the-art appliances.

One area had a counter surrounded by stools with a large bowl of fruit in the center of the counter top.

"Nice," he said, indicating the kitchen as Stephanie poured him a large glass of lemonade out of a pitcher and Ben sat on a counter stool.

"It's amazing how much work you can do on a house," Ben said, smiling, "when you don't have to pay mortgage payments every month."

Caro stared at Ben. "Then you know why I'm here?"

"Oh, sure, about the house," Stephanie said, still smiling. She sat down on another bar stool and slid her husband a large glass of ice water and cradled a second in her hands.

"Sit, enjoy your drink. We can talk about it," Ben said. "We've worked with banks before. In fact, I worked at Idaho's largest bank before I was laid off three years ago. I know how the system works."

"Yeah, you're here to get the house into shape to be sold," Stephanie said. "Right?"

Caro stared at her and then at her husband while nodding. Usually someone about to be kicked out of their home would be angry. These two just seemed pleased that he was here like they never had guests. He had to be careful about what he said. These two were clearly nuts.

Caro sat on the offered bar stool and took a deep sip from his lemonade. It tasted wonderful. The perfect drink for this kind of hot day.

"So tell me?" he asked, taking another sip and then putting the glass down on the counter. "Why aren't you two upset that your home is about to be sold out from under you?"

"Oh, it's not going to be," Ben said, smiling. Then he turned to Stephanie. "Which house on the street do you think we should have cleaned up and sold next?"

"Oh, the Benson's old place of course," Stephanie said. "That garage door damage just isn't doing the look of the neighborhood any good at all."

Caro just stared at her. He was right. She *was* nuts, completely nuts.

Ben turned to Caro. "You saw the house two doors down?"

Caro nodded. "Sure I did, but that's not the address on my paperwork. This is the address."

"Oh, I know that," Ben said. "But that's the place you are going to have your clean-up crews go and fix up and paint and let your company sell. Stephanie can even help them pick out colors, can't you dear?" Ben said.

"I'm really good at colors," Stephanie said, nodding and smiling.

"And why would I do that?" Caro asked, now starting to worry that these two might really be dangerous.

"You got a mortgage, Mr. Rosefield?"

"I do," he said.

"And when you saw us in this wonderful home, even doing painting, what did you think?"

"That there had been a massive screw-up somewhere."

"Exactly," Ben said, still smiling like he had just won the lottery. "You thought we had been paying our mortgage regularly for years and some bank somewhere had taken advantage of us. Right?"

"I did," Caro said. "Is that the case?"

"Of course not," Ben said, laughing. "We haven't paid a cent of mortgage for over three years now, and have no intention of ever paying again. In truth, we own this house completely."

"We're just trying to get the rest of the homes along Bryant Street cleaned up," Stephanie said. "We want to get some new neighbors, get things back to normal on our little street of dreams."

Caro wanted to call it more like a street of nightmares and nut-balls, but he didn't say anything. The lawyers were going to have a field day with this one.

"And you and your company would really help out if you would clean up that mess two doors down," Ben said.

Caro just shook his head. "I don't think you understand completely. I'm here for *this* house."

"Oh, we understand completely," Ben said. "But let me show you something. Remember, I worked for a major bank in their mortgage funding area for ten years. I know how all this works."

He climbed off the bar stool and indicated Caro should follow him.

Caro wasn't sure if he should or make a bolt for the front door, but decided he needed to understand just what these people thought they could do to stay mortgage free here. That way he could let his company lawyers know the scam these two crazies were trying to pull.

THREE

BEN LED HIM through the entry way and off the living room into a large side office with a huge computer system with at least five large monitors.

"Ben makes us a lot of money here trading stocks," Stephanie said, smiling.

"I could teach you," Ben said to Caro. "If down the road you are interested in getting out of your job."

"Thanks," Caro said. "But show me why you are not concerned about why I am here."

"Glad to," Ben said, sitting down in a high-backed chair and indicating Caro should come around and stand beside him to watch.

"Sweetie," Ben said to Stephanie, "would you make sure of the address on the old Benson place?"

"Glad to," Stephanie said and turned and headed out the front door as Ben clicked his computer screens out of sleep mode.

On the screen was all the paperwork Caro had for this property and his trip here. Every bit of it, including the house paperwork, his flight times, rental car agreement.

Everything.

"We knew you were coming," Ben said, smiling. "It's why Stephanie made lemonade and we have steaks for the grill with corn and a salad if you want to stay for dinner."

Caro opened his mouth, but couldn't think of a thing to say, so he just closed it again and just kept staring at the paperwork on the main screen. More than anything now he wanted to run for the front door and maybe the closest police station, but his feet stayed planted beside Ben's chair.

Ben pulled up all the paperwork and history for his house on a second screen and pointed to it. "You see, your company bought this a year ago, but the reality is that the people they bought this house from didn't actually own it either."

Ben pointed at another area of the screen. "I changed that and put this house into the pool for your company so we could get you here today. We didn't know it would be you, of course. But someone from your company would come knocking on the door eventually. It took almost seven months, pretty fast these days."

"You put your own house in a foreclosure auction?" Caro asked, stunned. This guy really, really, really was crazy.

"Oh, sure," Ben said, his fingers dancing over the keys. "Actually, this property is owned by three other companies like yours as well. As I said, we're just trying to get the neighborhood cleaned up."

On one side screen the address and property description of 2761 Bryant Street showed that it was on three other foreclosure sales and notices.

"How can you do that?" Caro asked, his voice choking. "How is that even possible?"

Ben laughed. "As I said, I worked in this area of banking for a decade. I was their computer tech, so they figured I wasn't needed when they downsized. It is stunningly easy in this mess of foreclosures to shift properties around."

"And the state records and recording?"

Ben laughed even harder and pulled up the state records showing that the home Caro was in was actually owned by four different companies and also Ben and Stephanie Davis. It showed Ben and Stephanie as not having a lien on the property at all.

Caro leaned against the chair. "This is crazy," he said. "You are crazy."

"Not really," Ben said. "Just call us the neighborhood clean-up committee and we have drafted your help. I could buy the homes myself and fix them up, but to be honest, I'm having more fun getting companies like your employers to do it for me."

At that moment Stephanie came back in the front door. "Wow, it's hot out there. We need to send the painters home."

"Address first," Ben shouted to her.

"Twenty-seven-thirty-seven," she said and then went back outside and closed the door.

Ben typed in the address and brought up all the paperwork for the property. It showed the property had been sold to First Trust and Loan two months ago.

"Time for a little trading around."

As Caro watched, his mind trying to grasp what he was seeing, Ben's fingers flew over his keyboard and within ten minutes Caro's company owned that property and it was the address on the work order he had. Caro's company had exchanged an equal value property to First Trust in a small town outside of Boise.

And Ben and Stephanie's house was no longer Caro's problem. The lien his company thought they had on it vanished as quickly as a few keystrokes, along with all the filing paperwork, purchase agreements, and state filings.

Caro stood up straight and tried to take a deep breath to clear his head. It almost worked. "I think you just broke about fifty laws."

"More like a hundred," Ben said, smiling. "But there is no way of tracing any of it and trust me, in this world, who is going to care that a few properties got switched around?"

"I'm sure someone can trace it if they wanted," Caro said.

Ben chuckled. "The banks these days can't even find the paperwork on a large percentage of the homes they actually do own. You know that."

Caro didn't want to nod, but he did. Ben was right. Mortgage paperwork was a mess in the best of times.

"So you made up the lien on this property out of whole cloth?" Caro asked.

"I sure did," Ben said. "We had this place paid off five years ago."

"And just to get my company here in your neighborhood to clean up other properties to make your street nicer?"

"You got it," Ben said, smiling. "We got a guy showing up here in a week from a savings and loan out of Utah. But since you made it first, you get the worst of the houses along the street. Trust me, the Bensons didn't go easily when they left."

"So what makes you think I'll go along with you?" Caro asked.

"For a start, you have no evidence of anything different," Ben said.

"Except for the original paperwork in my car," Caro said. "And the files back in my home office."

"I already printed off all the new work orders for you with the new address and Stephanie replaced them in your car while you were in here." Ben pointed at the screen. "I've changed all your companies official records. They think they own the house down the street and that's where you should be going."

"You've thought of everything except how to keep me quiet," Caro said, now feeling more annoyed than anything else.

Ben hit a key and on one of the previously dark screens an image of Caro's home in Portland came up.

"That's a nice place," Ben said.

"You wouldn't?" Caro asked, stunned.

"I wouldn't want to," Ben said. "Honestly, I wouldn't. And I wouldn't except as a last resort. But you've seen what I can do. I would rather have your help with making our street beautiful again."

Caro knew exactly what the man could do. All the years of making those payments could vanish in a few keystrokes. Caro would spend years trying to dig himself out of a mess that Ben could create in two minutes.

Caro had heard of it happening to other poor souls and he had no desire to be one of them.

And no one would believe his story of a mad hacker putting his own home in foreclosure to help clean up his neighborhood. That was just too crazy to even try to explain.

Ben shut off his computers and stood, pushing Caro back toward the kitchen. "Come on, let me get you something more to drink and we can sit and talk and Stephanie can work on that salad after she sends the painters on their way. After that I can put on the steaks."

Caro took another long drink from the cool lemonade. Then he dropped onto the stool and looked at Ben who had returned to his stool and was smiling.

"You really are crazy," Caro said.

Ben shrugged. "One person's craziness is another's sanity. You can't tell me you think this banking and home mortgage mess is sane. I'm just trying to clean it up a little."

"None of this makes any sense," Caro said. "Not one bit of it. You could have changed the work orders before I got here, sent me to that other house first."

Now Ben was really smiling and nodding as Stephanie came in and joined them. "I could have. You are right."

He looked at Stephanie and smiled. "He figured it out."

"I knew he would," Stephanie said, going to the sink and washing her hands.

"So why didn't you?" Caro asked.

Stephanie poured herself a glass of lemonade and put the pitcher back into the fridge.

"You want to tell him," Ben said to her.

"Because of your daughters," she said. "They need their father to be home."

Caro stood, pushing the stool back, panic ramping up and his heart pounding. "What do you know about my daughters?"

Ben for the first time looked serious. "I needed to know as much as I can about a man I'm going to offer a job to."

"You hate this travel," Stephanie said, moving over with the glass of lemonade and sitting down on a stool next to Caro. "Your daughters and your wife hate having you travel so much. It's all over your oldest daughter's Facebook page and in the e-mails your wife sends to her parents and to you when you are traveling."

"You can get to all of that?" Caro asked, his head spinning.

"You would be surprised what Ben can do," Stephanie said, smiling at her husband.

The First Two Cold Poker Gang Novels
Available at your favorite booksellers.

"Not any more I wouldn't," Caro said.

"So I've been planning on getting into real estate in the Portland area," Ben said, "and I need someone who knows houses, knows the area, to run my Oregon branch."

"You get to stay home with your children," Stephanie said.

"I'll pay off your home as a signing bonus and double your salary," Ben said.

"And if I don't agree?" Caro asked.

"We have corn, steaks, salad, and you go back to work tomorrow on that house two doors down. It's just an offer, nothing more."

"Actually," Stephanie said, "we'd like you to get that fixed up before you quit your current job."

"And why would I quit one job to do the same job with you?" Caro asked, trying to keep the anger out of his voice.

"It wouldn't be exactly the same job," Ben said, smiling.

"So what exactly would it be?"

At this point Caro was convinced, completely convinced, that he was facing two of the crazier people he had ever had the misfortune to run into. And every part of his brain said he needed to get out of that house quickly.

Stephanie was beaming and Ben's smile couldn't get any bigger.

Two fruitcakes. They were both nuts. Caro stood and backed a step away from the counter. Now even with air-conditioning he was sweating.

"This was Stephanie's idea," Ben said.

"I thought of it after we watched the Bensons get evicted," she said. "We liked them."

Ben nodded. "Yeah, good people. So I decided I could use the money we have, plus some money from the banks that I can get access to, to work to keep people in their homes."

"He's made a lot of money in stocks," she said, smiling.

Ben laughed. "I'm good at shorting bank stocks at exactly the right time."

"So we want you to meet with families who are about to be evicted," Stephanie said.

"I'll buy up their mortgage if you say they are solid people," Ben said. "You figure out what they can really afford and we'll set that up for them to pay. Make sure they stay in their home and the bank doesn't make a profit from their hardship."

"Can I think about it?" Caro asked, taking another step back. These two weren't just nuts, they were living in a fairy tale land.

"Of course," Ben said. "Take all the time you like. The job is yours if you want it."

"Thanks," he said, and turned for the door.

The heat hit him in the face like a slap and he made it to his car and got it started as fast as he could, getting the air-conditioning running. On the seat where he had left them was the paperwork he had brought from Oregon, but now the address was two doors down the street.

An address he never would have questioned an hour before.

FOUR

HE HEADED the big rental up Bryant Street until he found a shady place to park out of sight of good old Ben and Stephanie.

Then leaving the car running, he grabbed up his cell phone and hit speed dial. Denise at the home office in Portland answered. She was one of the best there was at computers and tracking housing paperwork. If anyone on the planet could find records that had been tampered with, it was Denise.

"I need you to pull up some paperwork on a house here," Caro said. "I want to make sure everything is in order before I move one more step on it."

"Smart thinking," Denise said. "You never know in these days.

"You got that right," Caro said.

Over the next thirty minutes, with the air-conditioning blowing on his face, he had her search every record the company had on the house on Bryant Street in Boise, Idaho.

No sign of tampering, no sign of anything different. The address he needed to work on was the empty house with the damaged garage door. The company had bought it eight months before at auction.

"Looks all square to me," Denise said finally. "State filing is all confirmed as well. We own it all fair and square."

He thanked her and hung up, then sat staring down Bryant Street.

Ben had been for real, or the entire thing had been an ugly heat vision. Or Caro really had fallen into the *Twilight Zone.*

Right now he needed to believe that Ben and Stephanie were for real. That they were two people with more money and skills than sense who just wanted to help people.

He hit speed dial again on his phone and this time got his wife.

"Wow, this is a pleasant surprise," Mary said.

"Where are you at?"

"Picking up Cindie," she said. "I got ten minutes before she gets out of school. Something wrong? You sound stressed."

"Sort of am," Caro said.

Then, as he had done with everything since they met, he told her what had happened with Ben and Stephanie.

"They want to save people's homes for them?" she asked after he had finished giving her the story, job offer and all. Everything but the threat against their house.

After working with Denise in his home office, Caro was convinced Ben would never do that unless really, really pushed. He didn't need to. He could cover his tracks completely and make anything Caro said look like a nut job talking. So Mary didn't need to worry about that happening. Caro had no thoughts of pushing.

"It sure seems that way," Caro said.

"He's really that good on computers?"

"He's the best I have ever seen," Caro said.

"And you would be at home and getting twice your salary?" she asked.

He could hear the excitement in her voice. He had no doubt which way she was going to go.

And now that he had stopped and thought about it and proved to himself that Ben could do what he seemed to appear to do, Caro was starting to like the idea more and more.

"It seems that way," Caro said. "It would be nice to be home with you and the girls every night."

"It would be wonderful," Mary said, her voice almost breathless as she said that. "But can these two afford to do what they are saying they want to do?"

"I have a hunch that Ben can do pretty much what he wants," Caro said. "But I will check to make sure."

At that moment in the background his daughter Cindie climbed into the car and Mary said hi and told her to get buckled in.

Caro looked down the hot neighborhood street and wished beyond anything that he was there with them.

Sometimes a guy has to take a chance when given to him, no matter how crazy that chance was.

"Mary," he said. "I think I'm going to go back and talk with them again."

"Oh, that would be so wonderful if this worked out," she said. "Good luck. Say goodbye to daddy."

Cindie said in the background, "Bye, Daddy. Hurry home."

And with that Mary hung up.

Caro was again alone in the air-conditioning of his rented car sitting on a hot street in a town he never wanted to visit again.

FIVE

HE SAT THINKING for another five minutes, running everything through his mind, then headed back toward Ben and Stephanie's home.

He stood in the heat once again and rang their bell.

And again both of them answered with wide smiles and invited him in and got him seated in their kitchen with a wonderful-tasting glass of lemonade in his hands.

"I talked to my wife and did some research on just how good you are at changing the paperwork."

"He's good, isn't he?" Stephanie said.

"Very good," Caro said. "My company has one of the best computer

people I know and she couldn't find a thing wrong with your paperwork on the Benson house up the street."

Ben only nodded.

"But if I did agree to work for you, I would need a few assurances."

"Go on," Ben said.

"I'll need to know you have the money to do all of this," Caro said.

"Fair enough," Ben said. "Stephanie, do you mind if I show Mr. Rosefield our accounts later?"

"Not at all," Stephanie said. "It's a logical request since he has a family to protect."

"And you'll do this all aboveboard?" Caro asked. "Last thing my daughters would need would be to have their father sent to jail."

"Ninety-nine percent of the time," Ben said. "But I have to be honest with you, I'm not going to feel bad helping a bank help a family stay in their home. And that might take a little computer hacking, but no theft. That much I can promise."

"No theft, ever?"

"Ever," Ben said. "I couldn't sleep if I did. Like cheating on my taxes. Not worth losing the sleep."

"And if he did I'd make him pay for it as well," Stephanie said, smiling.

"And she would, too," Ben said. "It's why I did the property trade so your company would be out no money and neither would the owner of the Benson place."

Caro nodded. He could live with a little computer hacking for the right cause.

They talked for another thirty minutes and Ben and Stephanie filled in all his questions better than he had hoped, actually.

He was convinced they were crazy. Crazy to even try something this stupid.

But he was starting to like their kind of crazy and for the first time in years he felt excited about the coming work he would be doing.

Finally, he had one more question. "You have a guy coming from Utah next week to do the same thing there?"

"We hope so," Stephanie said. "Someone has to do this."

"So all this was nothing more than a giant job interview, right?"

"Basically," Ben said, smiling. "It's going to take a certain type of person to do what we are hoping to do. So we need to run each of you through this to see how each of you react."

"And I passed?" Caro asked. "You're still offering me the job?"

"It is yours," Ben said, extending his hand

"You know, you both are crazy," Caro said, shaking Ben's hand and smiling for the first time in the day. "But I guess I am as well."

"Let's hope you are the first of many crazies to come," Ben said.

"This is the *Twilight Zone*, right?" Caro asked. "Rod Serling is standing in the corner, smoking, talking about how sometimes it takes ordinary people to help out other ordinary people."

Stephanie and Ben both laughed.

"Nope," Stephanie said. "This is Bryant Street, a street like every other street in the country, where good families live and magic can sometimes happen."

Caro raised his glass of lemonade in a toast. "Rod Serling himself could not have said it better."

BAD BEAT

A COLD POKER GANG MYSTERY

DEAN WESLEY SMITH

USA TODAY BESTSELLING AUTHOR

The Cold Poker Gang consists of a group of retired Las Vegas Police detectives getting together once a week to play cards and work to solve cold cases.

Retired Detectives Bayard Lott and Julia Rogers stand at an unmarked grave in the desert, about ready to close a thirty-year-old cold case of a missing woman.

But what appears from that grave keeps their case very much open, and shines a light on many other cold cases.

Another twisted mystery that only the Cold Poker Gang can solve.

BAD BEAT
A Cold Poker Gang Novel

PART ONE
First Bad Beat

PROLOGUE

March 3rd, 1987
Las Vegas, Nevada

BECKY PENN TIED her long brown hair back away from her face and laughed as her mom stood in their bathroom door, arms crossed over her chest, the worried look on her face that Becky saw so much from her.

Her mom had raised her since their father had left when Becky was three. The two of them were more like sisters at times and Becky loved that.

Becky was dressed in a light skirt, a new blouse she had just bought, and had on sandals, since the weather was already starting to warm up.

Becky's mom had already changed from her nursing scrubs into a light sweatshirt and jeans. She seldom wore shoes around the house and tonight was no exception.

"It's all right, mom," Becky said, smiling as she finished up and turned from the mirror. "Paul and I are headed to a party just off the strip. I'm going to meet him there."

"I wish you wouldn't," her mom said, shaking her head.

"I know, I know," Becky said. "You don't like him."

"I'm not sure why you do," her mom said.

Becky laughed. Paul was a good guy who worked hard. And he was a very gentle soul. Becky liked that about him.

Becky kissed her mother lightly on the cheek as she went past and out into the hallway of the small two-bedroom toward the front door. "You worry too much."

"Sometimes I wish you worried more," her mom said.

Then both of them laughed. That exchange had happened for every date Becky had ever gone on from a freshman in high school and all the way through four years at UNLV. It made them both feel better.

"Don't wait up," Becky said.

A minute later she was in her red two-door Toyota and headed out toward the Strip.

It was the last time anyone saw her.

She just simply vanished.

And just like so many other missing persons, after no leads came up, her case went cold.

Almost thirty years cold.

ONE

April 10th, 2015
Las Vegas, Nevada

RETIRED DETECTIVE Bayard Lott ran a hand through his short white hair and sighed. They weren't supposed to find a body. Lott hated every time they did that. Finding a body was never the way they wanted to close missing person's cases.

But more often than not, it was exactly how they closed them.

"Looks like we found Becky," Retired Detective Julia Rogers said.

Julia stood beside Lott staring down at the skeleton that was slowly emerging from the desert sand and dirt where it had been buried for twenty-eight years, as far as they could tell.

Lott didn't want to watch, but he felt he had no choice.

Beside him, Julia had on a light white blouse and a sports bra under it. She wore jeans and tennis shoes and a wide-brimmed white golf hat to keep the intense sun off her face.

Lott had on a short-sleeved dress shirt, jeans, tennis shoes and a wide-brimmed Panama hat. They had expected to spend time in the sun in the desert to the north of Las Vegas, so even though it was still early spring, they were both smeared with sunscreen that smelled like they belonged on a beach instead of out in the desert.

They might have looked silly and smelled funny, but he was in his sixties and Julia in her late fifties and they were smart enough to take no chances with the heat and sun of the desert. At their age, too much sun did not do well on either of them.

And besides, they were both past the age of caring that much about what other people thought of how they looked.

The open grave in front of them was being carefully worked by a couple of Las Vegas police's best forensic lab people. They were in white suits that had to be hot in the morning April sun in the desert. And they were being very careful to brush away sand from the bones of the body and then shovel it into containers to be sifted for personal effects or bits of cloth and hair.

Lott could visualize the wonderful college graduation picture of Becky Penn. She had been a beautiful woman with a promising future. She vanished on March 3rd, 1987, on her way to a party to meet her boyfriend.

It was her boyfriend, Paul Vaughan who had reported to Becky's mother three hours after they were supposed to meet that Becky had not shown up. He had called concerned that Becky had been sick or something.

Her mother filed a missing person's report that very night.

Nothing had ever come of it. The detective assigned to the case did some fine interviews, found nothing.

Lott didn't want to think of how many missing person's cases ended up that exact same way. During his active days on the force, most of his missing person's cases ended up cold and open. Las Vegas seemed to attract an unusual share of people either wanting to escape from others or people falling in with the wrong crowd.

On the surface Vegas was welcoming. And as long as a tourist stayed in the normal tourist channels, it was a pretty safe town. But just below those channels, mostly driven by vast amounts of money and greed, was a very dangerous level.

Two months ago, Retired Detective Andor Williams, Lott's former partner, brought the thin file on Becky Penn's case to the weekly meeting of the Cold Poker Gang.

Lott loved the weekly sessions in his card room in his house. Retired detectives got together, played poker, and talked about cold cases. Then during the week between games, they worked the cold cases.

The Las Vegas Chief of Police had given the Cold Poker Gang special status to carry badges and guns because they had solved so many cold cases and wanted no credit for any of it.

For the retired detectives, it was just the sense of feeling valued that mattered and continuing at their own pace, without paperwork, the job they had loved for decades.

Lott flat loved everything about being part of the Cold Poker Gang and couldn't imagine his life without it. He had no idea what he would be doing.

When Julia joined the group, she had retired from Reno because of a shattered bone in her leg where she had been shot. She had moved to Vegas to be near her daughter, Jane, who was going to UNLV.

So far Julie was been the only woman in the gang, but in a year or so, two of Las Vegas's best women detectives would be retiring. Both wanted to take a couple months vacation and then join the group.

Now the Cold Poker Gang often had seven or eight people at the table on a Tuesday night. Made his wonderful poker room a lot of fun. And sometimes noisy, which Lott felt gave life to his home every week.

There were eleven official members and every active detective on the force liked helping them.

At any given moment, the gang might have eight or nine cold cases they were working in some fashion or another, often in pairs.

"Let's sit in the car for a while," Julia said, turning from the grave.

Lott agreed to that idea. Not only did he not want to watch the bones of a beautiful young girl come into the open, but the sun was getting warmer by the minute.

And there was absolutely nothing they could do to help in that shallow hole. Getting Becky Penn's remains out of that hole would take time and painstaking work. Lott was just glad he wasn't doing the work, especially in one of those white suits they wore these days.

Lott got his white Cadillac SUV started and the air-conditioning running as Julia dug them both out a cold bottle of water from the ice chest sitting on the back seat.

Then they just sat in silence for a moment, drinking, cooling down and watching the two men in the shallow hole work.

Lott was always surprised at how wonderful cold water tasted after being out in the Nevada sun for a while.

"I can't believe we found her," Julia said after a moment.

"We're still not one hundred percent that it is her," Lott said.

And they weren't, but that was just a technical issue now. They had figured out where she was buried exactly from notes in a journal left by her boyfriend, Paul Vaughan, when he killed himself in 1997, ten years after Becky vanished.

From what they could tell when they got the journal, still stored with Paul's

things by his sister, Jennifer Season. She had found the journal while she was packing to move and read it and called them. The journal basically told the story about how Paul and Becky had gotten into a fight and he had killed her.

The journal went on to give exact directions to where he had buried her and then what he had done to cover his crime.

Lott had found the writing creepy. Impassionate while being angry.

Lott had been upset that the guy was dead. But if he hadn't been dead, there was no telling if they ever would have solved Becky's cold case. They were lucky in a couple of ways. That he was dead and that his sister had just stored what few things he owned in boxes in her basement.

But something felt off to both Julia and Lott. And Lott couldn't put his finger on it at all.

First, they had no idea why a killer like Paul would write down what he had done, then give exact directions to the grave.

And his sister had told them that Paul hated to write anything, let alone in a journal.

But it seemed, at least on the surface, that Paul had started the journal when he and Becky started dating and they had confirmed with Becky's mother some of the dates and times in the journal as best as she could remember.

So it all seemed real enough.

But to Lott the operative word was "seemed." It seemed right but didn't feel right.

The second thing that puzzled him was what had happened to Becky's red Toyota? The car had simply vanished and Paul made no mention of it in his strange journal. And he should have. Getting rid of that car had to be a lot harder than burying her in the desert.

Something was off on all of this, but darned if Lott could figure out what was bothering him about it all.

Then, in front of them, one of the two men working in the shallow grave in white suits stood up, turned and waved for Lott and Julia to come over.

Then both men climbed out of the shallow grave and one headed for their vehicle, pulling off his white suit as he went.

"Something went wrong," Julia said as both she and Lott climbed out of the car.

The other man who had waved them over had pulled off the top of his white suit as well and was working on a bottle of water. His face was covered in sweat.

"What did you find?" Lott asked.

The guy just pointed for them to look into the grave and kept drinking.

It took a moment for Lott to see it, but then he did.

Nowhere in any report did it say that Becky had three arms.

"There's another body under her," Julia said softly.

"Shit," Lott said. "Just shit."

TWO

April 12th, 2015
Las Vegas, Nevada

JULIA LOVED the lunches with Lott and Andor. Especially when it came to discussing cases. But she had a hunch she wasn't going to like today's topic at all.

Lott set the bucket of Kentucky Fried Chicken on his kitchen table while Julia pulled out three bottles of water from the fridge. Andor had just parked outside in the driveway and was going to join them for lunch.

The smell of the chicken filled Lott's remodeled kitchen. In the remodel, he had put in the best counters, all new cabinets and flooring, all in tones of brown. And stainless steel new appliances. But he said the floor plan of the kitchen was exactly as it had been when he and his wife had lived here.

Julia loved what he had done with the kitchen. It felt comfortable.

And the wood-topped table sat in a sunny nook and looked out over the yard and desert plants outside of Lott's home, giving anyone sitting at the table a sense of comfort and serenity.

Lott's wife of thirty years had died of cancer almost four years ago. He told Julia that it wasn't until she walked into his life that he could ever imagine enjoying the company of another woman. But now he did.

And she was enjoying being with him, the first real relationship she had had in a very long time.

She loved Annie, his daughter, and Annie really liked Julia as well. Annie was a professional poker player and the girlfriend and partner of Doc Hill, the best poker player in the world at the moment. They were a power couple if Julia had ever seen one.

And combine Annie and Doc with Doc's best friend, Fleet, and there was nothing they couldn't do. And they had the money to do it as well.

They also spent a lot of time working with law enforcement in various ways. Since Annie was a former detective and

Doc and Fleet had the money and desire to help, it turned out to be a good match for many things.

Julia finished putting the bottles of water on the table as Andor slammed his car door outside. She and Lott and Andor, Lott's former partner back on the force before they both had retired to take care of sick wives, formed a team in the Cold Poker Gang. They all just felt like they got more done with three of them working together.

And outside of the nights with the Cold Poker Gang playing cards, the three of them often met over KFC in Lott's kitchen to talk over cases.

Today the topic was Becky Penn's cold case and the other bodies in her grave. Julia had a hunch they would be off the case, but she hadn't said that to Lott.

And he had said nothing either, although she could tell he was angry, very angry, that there were other bodies in that grave.

Lott spread around three paper plates and Julia got some forks for pulling the hot chicken apart and some spoons for the sides that came with the bucket. They didn't often eat much of the sides. All three of them just loved the fresh chicken.

Andor came in the back door, his solid frame and balding head moving like a bull. He had a cold towel around his neck and was sweating. Andor was almost square with his wide shoulders seeming to always be slightly hunched. But he had a mind that didn't miss much and she liked him a great deal.

Andor's wife had died of cancer about the same time as Lott's wife. They both had retired to take care of them, so the Cold Poker Gang allowed them to keep going with the job they both loved.

Julia handed Andor a fresh hand towel to wipe off his face and head and neck, then she sat next to Lott at the table.

Andor dropped some files at the back of the table and all three of them dug into the chicken.

Finally, after pretty much demolishing their first pieces and starting on seconds, Julia couldn't take it any longer.

She looked at Andor. "Well, was one of them Becky Penn?"

When the other bodies were found in Becky's grave, the case had reverted back to the regular younger detectives. By the end of the day, the techs doing the digging had found a total of four bodies in that grave, all stacked on one another with a very thin layer of dirt between them.

And all of them had been killed with a blow to the head that clearly caved in the skull bone.

From what Julia had heard, the techs were now doing ground radar sweeps around the grave to see if others were buried close by.

Paul Vaughan's journal had led them to the location, but he had said nothing about killing and burying other women.

This entire case just was off.

Way off.

But Julia had no idea at all how to even find the next lead.

Andor nodded, wiping chicken grease off his mouth with a paper towel. "It was Becky on top," Andor said. "Confirmed by remnants of what she was wearing, hair color, and the remains of her ID buried with her. They will run some DNA tests, but no one is doubting it is her."

"And the other three?" Lott asked.

"They don't have a clue," Andor said. "But they are treating all four as live murder cases at the moment."

Julia shook her head. All were very cold cases if they had been buried under Becky's body.

Andor just looked at them. "We're out of this one for now. You both know that, don't you?"

Julia knew they were. As long as the younger detectives considered the bodies open and live murder cases, there was nothing anyone retired in the Cold Poker Gang could do.

And actually, by doing anything, they might jeopardize the entire existence of the Cold Poker Gang.

They worked cold cases.

Period.

That was the firm rule the Chief of Police had put on them.

Becky's case was now officially a live murder case. Along with the other three.

The Cold Poker Gang was done with them.

Lott was nodding, and not looking happy.

Julia just sat there, not sure if she was even interested in another piece of chicken.

"This day just sucks," Lott said.

"Yeah, it does," Andor said. "But we have to give the hotshot young detectives a crack at this first. Remember, we were young once as well."

"Speak for yourself," Julia said. "I'm still young, thank you very much."

She felt just as upset about this as they did, but she knew the rules, just as they did.

Lott and Andor both laughed.

Julia smiled. "Not sure how I should take that laughing."

"Oh, oh," Andor said, winking at Lott.

"So what are the files?" Julia asked, indicating the folding files that Andor had at the top of the table. She had a hunch they were the active files of the four cases. But she wanted Andor to tell her for sure.

"I brought them for storage here," he said, starting into another piece of chicken.

Lott laughed at that and took a second piece of chicken. Then after a bite and wiping off his hands, he had Julia hand the files to him.

First Three Cold Poker Gang Novels
Available at your favorite booksellers.

Without looking at their contents, he stood and put them in an empty cabinet above the fridge.

Storage.

"All four files for the bodies in the grave?" Julia asked, just wanting to make sure.

Andor nodded. "I'll get more from downtown and update them as the young hotshots find information."

Lott laughed again and sat down and took another bite of chicken.

"And if they solve the cases?" Julia asked, smiling as she also took another piece of the wonderful-smelling chicken.

"Wonderful," Lott said. "But I'm betting anything Paul Vaughan didn't do all four, or even Becky for that matter."

"No bet," Andor said, working at another piece of chicken.

"And if they don't solve them, then we go to work on the cases," Lott said. "But that's going to be a year or more down the road I'm afraid."

Julia agreed. She hated it, but she agreed.

Andor nodded. "So the day officially sucks. We are officially fired from these cases."

"We move on," Julia said, nodding and biting into another piece of chicken.

"We move on," Andor said, wiping chicken juice from his face again.

"There are no shortages of cold cases for us to solve," Julia said as she chewed.

"Amen to that," Lott said.

Julia knew that was the truth. But she just hated failing, hated having a case taken from her, hated everything about this.

The Cold Poker Gang hadn't really solved a cold case. They had just found more murders that, more than likely, would turn into cold cases in a year or two.

She knew that all three of them hated failing. They didn't volunteer their time in their retirement to fail.

But sometimes it happened. Sometimes even the Cold Poker Gang failed.

Or, as they say in poker, you can't win every hand, even on good nights.

But down the road, way down the road, they just might get to play this hand all over again.

And when that happened, they would be ready.

THREE
One year and six months later…

September 16th, 2016
Las Vegas, Nevada

LOTT FOUND IT still too hot out to park his car and walk to the entrance of the Bellagio Hotel and Casino. His car said it was a couple degrees over a hundred. So once again he used valet parking. He had more than enough money to not have to walk through heat if he didn't have to. A simple pleasure in life.

Andor had called this dinner meeting for the team at the Bellagio Café, one of their favorite places. The café had just about anything a person could want at any time of the day or night. And it had plant-surrounded booths and tables that allowed for privacy.

On top of that, it was far enough from the casino that all the noise there was just background. Yet it felt alive and at his age, Lott liked feeling alive.

As Lott handed the valet a tip and started toward the hotel entrance, Julia pulled up in her SUV. He waved and pointed that he would be just inside the door and she nodded.

He had no doubt that over the last few years he had fallen in love with Julia, something he never thought possible after his wife's death. And Julia was in love with him as well. He just couldn't imagine why anyone who looked as good as she did with her bright green eyes, long brown hair, and incredible brain would find an older guy like him attractive. But thankfully, she did.

And most nights they stayed in her wonderful condo. They had talked about her moving in with him. And Annie, his daughter, had thought that would be a wonderful idea, but so far nothing had pushed them to that.

As Julia came though the door, he gave her a kiss. She had her hair pulled back and tied and wore a light blouse with a sports bra under it and tan slacks and sandals. She smelled wonderful. She always did.

"Good workout?" Lott asked.

"Still taking it a little easy because of the heat outside," Julia said. "I'll ramp it up more as we go into the cooler season."

Lott nodded. Julia belonged to a gym a few blocks off the strip and unless they were busy, she always found time to workout, usually running on the treadmill.

He did some exercise, but not as much as she did. Mostly he walked when the heat allowed and did standard sit-ups and push-ups every morning, same as he had been doing for over forty years.

It made him feel like his day was starting if he kept that routine up.

They headed through the sounds of the bells from slot machines and the low hum of talking from the people flowing toward one part or another of the vast casino and hotel. Even late at night this place never seemed to be short of visitors. But now, around the dinner hour, the place was almost jammed.

Lott enjoyed that as well. He enjoyed people and being around people, he had come to realize.

"Any chance we might run into Annie and Doc here tonight?" Julia asked.

"Possible," Lott said. "I could check the poker room to let them know we are here after we get settled."

Annie and Doc often played in the larger nightly tournaments here when in town. But Lott couldn't honestly remember if they were scheduled to be in town or not right now. Doc and his business partner, Fleet, had a private jet that took them all over the country to major tournaments. So Lott never knew for sure if his daughter was in town or not.

Lott had asked Fleet once if Doc made enough to justify flying to poker tournaments in a private jet. Fleet had just laughed and said that Doc and Annie made enough on most tournaments and ring games to pay for three jets to get there and back.

Sometimes it was hard for Lott to get it through his head that his retired detective daughter was now a jetsetter in the professional poker world. But Lott sure enjoyed the help Doc and Annie and Fleet gave them on some cases. Having those sorts of resources behind solving a cold case never hurt.

And from what Annie and Doc and Fleet often said to him, they loved helping out. They also had their own network where they worked with police and the FBI on different crimes at times. Having vast sums of money and the willingness to throw it at a case often made friends with budget-constrained law enforcement agencies.

He and Julia had just gotten settled in a large booth near the back of the café when Andor came toward them. He was wearing his normal dress shirt, sleeves rolled up, and he was sweating. Lott just shook his head, since Andor also had more than enough money to valet park his car, but refused to do so, no matter how hot it was. Instead he chose to hike from the parking lot.

Julia handed him a glass of cold water and a few napkins as he slid into the booth across from them.

"Thanks," he said, then downed half the glass of water before dipping one of the napkins in the rest to wipe down his face with cold water.

A nice waiter named Stan got their drink orders and vanished.

"So what's the reason for this surprise dinner?" Julia asked a half second before Lott could.

They often came here when a case was active, or for late-night food after a Cold Poker Gang night. But at the moment they had no really active cases.

"We're back in the game," Andor said, smiling before finishing off his water.

Lott looked at his partner. He had no idea what game Andor was talking about.

Julia was looking as puzzled as he felt.

Andor just laughed. "Becky Penn. That name ring a bell?"

Lott felt a thrill run through his spine. "The chief released them to us?"

Andor nodded and smiled. "Officially all four murder cases have gone cold. Chief turned them over to us along with all the notes."

"Fantastic!" Julia said, clapping her hands together.

Lott felt the same way. Those poor souls had died thirty years ago. He just hoped that now they could do something about it and find out who killed and buried them in that grave in the desert.

But thirty years was a lot of cold.

FOUR

September 16th, 2016
Las Vegas, Nevada

THE BACKGROUND SOUNDS of the casino floated around them from the distance, most blocked by the walls of plants. Julia felt both excited and worried about now taking over the Becky Penn cold cases.

It had been a long time since Becky vanished and was killed. And clearly the other three under her in the grave had died before her. Leads often went very cold in that amount of time.

Very, very cold.

But she and Lott and Andor had been waiting for over a year to get these cases back. They knew the active detectives had made no headway. But that they had all expected, since brand new daily cases took most of the active detectives' time.

But for the three of them, these cases would be all they would do. And that excited her more than she wanted to admit.

No wonder Andor had called this meeting. He was excited as well.

They gave the waiter their dinner orders and then Julia pulled out her notebook and opened it to a clean page and looked first at Lott and then Andor.

Both were smiling.

The notebook was a symbol of starting a case for them.

"So where do we start with this monster elephant of a problem?" Julia asked.

"We start with what we know," Lott said.

Andor nodded.

So Julia started to write and talk. "First, we know Becky vanished without a trace headed to meet her boyfriend, Paul Vaughan. She was in a red Toyota which was never found."

"Right," Lott said. "And Paul Vaughan killed himself ten years later."

"Supposedly," Andor said.

Julia looked up at Andor and nodded. She had not thought to even question that when they caught this cold case the first time.

"Marking that down as the first unknown," she said. "Did he really kill himself? And if he didn't, who died and who killed them?"

"And he supposedly kept a journal of the dates with him and Becky," Lott said, "even though his sister said he hated to write."

Julia wrote all that down.

"Can we trust his sister on any of that?" Andor asked.

Julia wrote that down.

"He kept no other journal," Andor said, "even though we found three other women's bodies under Becky's body in the grave his journal led us to."

"I've always thought someone else planted that journal," Lott said.

Julia agreed completely and wrote that down as a second major unknown.

"Did they even come up with any names of the other three women in the grave?" Lott asked Andor.

Julia watched as Andor shook his head.

"They know they were killed before Becky," Andor said, "but not much before. The woman on the bottom was killed less than a year ahead of Becky, if that much. That's all we know."

"Did the active detectives check out other missing women from the same time?" Lott asked.

"Not well," Andor said. "Too many missing and not enough time for them."

Julia nodded and wrote that on her notes as well under unknown questions.

"The Toyota?" Lott said. "Where did it go?"

"That's always bothered me as well," Julia said as she wrote that under the unknown question area.

At that point dinner arrived, but Lott stood and pointed to his food. "Don't touch that. I'm going to see if Annie and Doc are in the poker room. We could use their computer people's help on some of this. Especially trying to track that car."

Julia smiled and put her notebook on the seat beside her to make room for her wonderful-smelling chicken fried steak. She had ordered corn on the cob with the steak and white gravy. Looking at the large plate of food, she realized she was really hungry.

So as Lott vanished, both she and Andor dug into their dinners.

It felt great to have this case back in their hands again.

Unfinished business they were all focused on finishing.

FIVE

September 16th, 2016
Las Vegas, Nevada

LOTT WAS HAPPY to see Annie, his daughter, standing off to one side of the poker room, her arms crossed across her chest just as her mother used to stand when focused on something. He always loved to watch Carol when she stood like that, and Annie was no exception.

Somehow he wondered how he and Carol had managed to bring up such a competent and wonderful daughter. Most of it had been Carol, since he had been working so much.

Even being in love with Julia didn't stop his missing Carol almost every day.

Doc was nowhere to be seen, but Annie found the game in front of her clearly fascinating.

Annie wore what she always wore in a poker room. A white blouse tucked into jeans. She usually had her long hair pulled back and tied away from her face and she always wore tennis shoes. She sometimes had a sweatshirt tied around her waist like a runner, in case she got stuck in a tournament sitting under an air-conditioning vent.

She was tall and thin and always looked completely in shape.

She was also now considered one of the best tournament poker players on the planet and clearly the best woman playing the game. And she was so charming and friendly, it seemed others almost loved giving her their chips.

As he started toward her, she looked up and gave him a beaming smile and pointed out of the poker room.

He stopped and turned around and she followed him out into the noisier, but actually more private area of slot machines.

She gave him a hug as she always did, then got right to the point, something he loved about his daughter, and that he had loved about her mother as well.

"What are you doing down here?"

"Julia and Andor and I are having dinner in the café," he said, smiling.

"Caught a good case, huh?" she asked, laughing.

She knew him and Julia and Andor far too well. And she loved the fact that he wasn't "moping" around the house anymore, as she called what he did for years after Carol died. And she really liked Julia, which made him happy as well.

Lott knew Annie sometimes missed being a detective and loved to help them when she could. And Doc and Fleet never missed an opportunity to help as well. So when he nodded they had caught a good case, her eyes lit up.

"Remember the Becky Penn case we lost to the young detectives over a year ago?" he asked.

"The ones with more bodies in the grave?" she asked, her eyes getting wide.

"We got all of it back today. All four cases."

"Oh, wow," she said. "Mind if I join you for dinner?"

"We would love it," Lott said. "But aren't you playing in a tournament tonight?"

"Doc's up in Boise helping out his grandfather and mother on something to do with family property," Julia said. "I was thinking of playing, but my head really wasn't in it. This sounds like a ton more fun."

"Then join the party," Lott said, taking his daughter by the shoulder and turning her toward the café.

"So you think Doc and my resources can help on this?" Annie asked as they walked.

Clearly she and Doc were a couple for life. They just hadn't gotten married yet, that Lott knew about. But he wouldn't have put it past them to have gotten married and not told anyone. They clearly worked as partners in just about everything.

"Becky Penn had a red Toyota that just vanished when she did," Lott said.

"We think that's one place your computer people could help."

"Any ID on the other three buried in the grave with her?"

"Nothing," Lott said as they got close to the table. "And that's another place I would love to have you help us. They were all women and young like Becky was. There were a lot of missing women during that time."

"Glad to help," she said. "If you buy me dinner."

He laughed as Annie slid in beside Andor and Lott took his place back in front of his steak and fries.

"You help us solve this, dear daughter, and I'll buy you dinner for six months."

"Deal," she said, laughing.

"I'll chip in," Julia said.

And with that, Lott knew their team had just gotten bigger. Annie and Doc and all their resources and computer people had just climbed on board.

And that gave them that much more chance of doing the impossible and tracking down this killer from thirty years ago.

SIX

September 16th, 2016
Las Vegas, Nevada

JULIA LOVED the fact that Annie and Doc and all the resources they had were on board this case. It was going to make things a lot easier and allow them to investigate a lot deeper to track down this killer.

Doc's best friend and business partner, Fleet, seemed to know computer people who could dig into things and get information Julia was pretty certain wasn't supposed to be gotten.

And it seemed that Doc and Fleet and Annie knew someone in all levels of governments in most western states. They even had the ear of the President of the United States thanks to their first case together. For two professional poker players and a businessman, the three of them had resources far beyond any normal police force.

And they weren't afraid to use them when they believed in the cause or the case.

Julia really enjoyed Annie as a person as well. Annie and Julia's daughter Jane had gotten to know each other and also liked each other. Which cleared up any family issues that Julia and Lott might have in their relationship.

Julia and Lott were both going slowly, but lately they had been talking about more. She wasn't sure what that more would entail just yet, but she wasn't going to go away.

And Lott wasn't going away from her either.

And she loved waking up in the morning with him beside her. She felt that started the day perfectly, no matter what she was doing.

After twenty minutes of talking and laughing as they all finished eating and Annie got some food as well, Andor turned the conversation back to the case.

Julia brought her notebook back up to the table beside her now-empty cherry pie plate and told Annie what they had talked about so far.

Annie nodded, listening, then said when Julia had finished, "Where can we help?"

"We have the Toyota license number and vin number," Andor said to Annie.

"Can your computer people have any chance of finding out where that car ended up thirty years ago?"

"We might be able to backtrack from there," Julia said.

"I'll get them on it early in the morning," Annie said. "Never know what those magicians with keyboards can find."

She turned to Lott. "Can you send me the details on the other three bodies, approximate age, approximate time of death, hair color, height, that sort of thing?"

Lott nodded. "I'll get it all out of the files and have it e-mailed to you before I go to bed tonight."

"I think we should be able to cross-check with computer programs," Annie said, "all the missing women from that time period to the details that we have and narrow it all down a great deal."

"Something not even the young detectives on the force had time to do," Andor said.

"No surprise," Annie said. "Not with the reduction in money and manpower and the increase in population and crime, those detectives are lucky to sleep at night."

Julia nodded at that.

"If we can narrow it down like that," Lott said, smiling at his daughter, "we can then do the leg work to see if we can find some similarities."

"I'd love to be a part of that field work," Annie said. "If you need me."

All three of them laughed and Annie smiled.

"I have a hunch we're going to need all the help we can get to solve this one."

"Amen to that," Andor said.

"We like a challenge, don't we?" Lott asked.

Julia and Annie and Andor all agreed to that.

But Julia knew this case was more than just a challenge. After thirty-plus years, it might turn out to be flat impossible. But the only way they would know was to dig in and tackle it.

SEVEN

September 17th, 2016
Las Vegas, Nevada

THE NEXT MORNING Julia took off to do her exercise at the gym and Lott headed home to change clothes and take a shower. He had clothes at Julia's, but he still liked his own shower and closet at home.

Over the last year, he had removed from the bedroom anything that would remind him of Carol. He had no intention of forgetting her, but she had wanted him to move on and after all these years since her death, he was doing his best to do just that.

And as Annie had said, "It was about damn time."

He had also moved his master bedroom to Annie's old room and turned his and Carol's old bedroom into a double-sided walk-in closet. He had had the work done secretly without telling Julia.

Neither of them wanted him to sell the house and move elsewhere because they both loved the kitchen and also the new poker room in the basement where the Cold Poker Gang met every week.

So if he wasn't going to sell the house, he had to make it comfortable for Julia.

He had also cleared out and stored all of Carol's things from the living room and dining room, and bought new furniture for there as well, including a large new big screen television, something Julia had commented on and liked.

It was his living room now, not the room where Carol had sat during her dying days.

One step at a time is what he told himself.

One step at a time.

He had just finished showering and getting dressed and was reading the morning paper at his kitchen table overlooking his yard when Annie called.

"We found where the Toyota ended up in 1987," she said before even saying hello.

"What happened to it?" he asked, his excitement climbing at the first real lead in this case since they found that diary, the one that they were all sure was fake and planted.

Last night before they left the café, they had divided the tasks they had. Andor was going to dig into the facts of Paul Vaughan's death. He had been Becky's boyfriend and the supposed owner of the diary.

Lott and Julia were going to dig into Paul Vaughan's sister some more and try to figure out when that diary could have been planted or if she did it.

Annie was going to work on the car with her and Doc's resources. She was also going to attempt to narrow down the number of missing persons that matched the other three bodies in the grave.

"It was sold in Reno," Annie said, "a week after Becky Penn went missing, off a used car lot there."

"Car lot still in existence?" Lott asked, not having much hope for the answer.

"It is," Annie said, almost laughing. "Original owner still has it as well. Doc is still working with his mother, but Fleet said he will have the jet at the airport in just over an hour if you and Julia want to make a little jaunt to Reno."

"Wonderful," Lott said. "Thanks, that will save a very long drive."

"And give Julia a chance to show you her old stomping grounds."

"I would never accuse Julia of stomping," Lott said, laughing.

Annie laughed as well. "Real good point. I'll keep everyone here digging on the other women in that grave. Fleet and his computer people are feeling challenged."

"That can mean nothing but good," Lott said.

"My thought exactly," Annie said. "Call me if you find anything."

"I'll call you one way or the other," Lott said. "Thanks."

"Safe trip, dad," Annie said, and hung up.

Lott called Julia and told her the plan and said he would pick her up at her apartment.

Less than two hours later he and Julia were boarding the private jet for the short hop up to Reno.

Lott really had no real hope of getting any useful information after thirty years. But in cold cases, you just never knew when or where a clue would come that would break the entire thing open.

And maybe this time figuring out how Becky Penn's car got to Reno and could be sold would be the one clue they needed.

But chances are it would be a dead end. But at least on this trip, they would be riding to the dead end in style.

EIGHT

September 17th, 2016
Reno, Nevada

THE PRIVATE JET was the ultimate in luxury travel. Large leather chairs, a table in one area between two chairs, and a flight attendant named June who looked to be about Annie's age.

Julia had met her a few times on different cases when Annie and Doc and Fleet had lent them use of the private plane. And Julie liked her a great deal. June had a smile and laugh that seemed to light up a room. She couldn't have been more than five-two and had long brown hair pulled back.

Besides the two pilots, both former Air Force fighter pilots, Julia and Lott and June were the people on the big plane. Julia decided a while back she didn't want to know how much it cost for them to "borrow" the plane. On just this short trip alone there were three very expensive salaried people, not counting the fuel and other costs of the plane.

She knew that Annie and Doc and Fleet were amazingly rich, but every so often she really understood just how rich.

She felt excited about going back to Reno. It had been years and she had kept in touch with her chief at the station every few months along the way. She had liked Reno, for the most part, but now she actually loved Las Vegas, and could never imagine moving back to the small town tucked against the mountains in Northern Nevada.

It seemed that the plane had barely left Las Vegas when they were on the ground in Reno. During the short time she and

Lott had talked about how to approach the car dealer.

She knew the place, knew it had a reputation of decent dealings, and as far as she could find, no complaints had been filed against the owner. But they both decided that they would stop in and talk to her captain first and get him on board and find out anything more about the dealership.

When they taxied into the private plane area of the airport, June told them that Fleet had a Cadillac SUV waiting for them. It was white, just like Lott's car they had driven to the airport. Same year and model, even.

"How does he do that?" Lott asked, shaking his head.

"Doc and Fleet keep two cars at the airport in all the major cities they go to," June said. "The pilots and I will be taking the other downtown to get some lunch, so call us when you are ready to head back."

At that Julia just laughed. "It will be at least a few hours."

As they climbed down the steps from the plane to the tarmac, Julia felt the difference in the air instantly. In Las Vegas, the air, even at ten in the morning had been thin and hot. Here, at eleven in the morning, the air felt like it had a little bite to it, even though the sun was shining on the mountains to the west.

It would be hot later in the afternoon and then cool off a great deal in the evening, something Vegas didn't do much. And the air here had a smell of pine and mountains while Vegas air always smelled of hot desert and sagebrush.

Julia and Lott's first stop was police headquarters and except for a few new young faces, it was as if she had never left. Everyone crowded around as she came in and gave her hugs and told her

how much the Vegas heat was clearly agreeing with her.

She introduced Lott to a number of the other detectives and then Norbert, the chief of police, came out of his office and gave her a hug as well and welcomed Lott.

Norbert was a solid man who stood about five-eight and had shoulders almost that wide. He had a slight gut on him now at fifty and a bald head, but Julia had no doubt he could take down anyone in the building.

He had a firm but friendly way of running things and his officers and staff seemed to go out of their way to make him happy when they could. She knew she had as well when working for him. He commanded respect and gave friendship in return. An amazing man, someone she called a friend.

A few minutes later they were sitting in his office and as Norbert often did, he got right to the point. "So what brings you two out of the big city and up to Reno?"

"Working a cold case," Julia said. "Thirty years cold."

"Your poker bunch?" Norbert asked, which surprised Julia.

Beside her Lott smiled.

"We call it the Cold Poker Gang," Julia said. "A bunch of retired detectives solving cold cases."

"I hear your track record is top notch," Norbert said, smiling. "The chief down there keeps me up on things and he asked me if I was all right with you still carrying your badge and gun and working unofficially with the gang. I sang your praises."

Julia felt herself blushing. "Thanks. I mean it."

"You folks ever want to start a branch up here in Reno, you let me know. I got a few more years before I retire and would love to be a part of that."

"Enough retired detectives around here?" Lott asked.

"Other areas and state cops from this area," Norbert said, nodding. "I have a hunch we might scrape together five or six who don't use walkers and want to have some fun working on cold cases without all the paperwork."

Lott and Julia both laughed at that. For Julia that was the best part of investigating, solving a case and giving the younger detectives the credit and the paperwork.

"When you are ready to roll," Lott said, "Some of us will come up and tell you how we do it."

"Perfect," Norbert said. "So how does your cold case link in here?"

Julia went through what they knew about the Becky Penn disappearance, about the other unidentified bodies, the delay, and now they had traced Becky's car to a dealership here called Bonanza Used Cars."

Norbert nodded. "Dewey Maxwell has had that place for forty years. Inherited it when he was twenty-two when his dad was killed in a hunting accident."

"Anything you can tell us about him?" Julia asked. "I never had any reason to do anything but drive by the place."

"No one has," Norbert said. "Dewey runs a very tight ship. All legal and above-board. Member of the chamber and Elks and has kids out of college. One of them is working with him now, from what I hear."

Julia was feeling a little hopeful. Maybe Dewey might be able to help them.

"Tell Dewey that I say hi," Norbert said.

"I will," Julia said. And with a hug for her former chief, she and Lott were headed out of her old headquarters.

It had felt odd to be back. A part of her felt like she had never left.

But most of her knew that her new life, one she loved more than any of her years in Reno, was beside Lott and in Las Vegas trying to help where she could.

That felt perfect for her. So as she walked out, she didn't even look back.

NINE

September 17th, 2016
Reno, Nevada

LOTT HADN'T BEEN surprised at how much Julia was loved in her old headquarters. Over the last few years getting to know her, he couldn't imagine anyone not liking her.

And her former chief, Norbert, clearly respected her and she felt the same for him. Lott had instantly liked the chief. A solid man who Lott had no doubt could be trusted completely on anything.

On the way to the car dealership, Lott and Julia had decided to just tell Dewey Maxwell the truth about what they were doing. After thirty years, it didn't seem to make any sense to try to hide any information from the man.

Lott didn't know what to expect from the dealership, but when they pulled in, he had still been surprised. It was a large place, covering acres along one side of the main highway to the south of Reno. It was well lit, the cars polished and clean, and the main building of the dealership looked almost new.

A second building held a number of repair bays and a bunch of mechanics.

"Wow, this place is nicer and bigger than I imagined it to be," Lott said.

"I think they have made a few improvements since I left," Annie said. "But still about the same size."

They headed through the slowly warming morning air and into the dealership. The inside had a dozen cars scattered around a polished floor showroom and at least four salesmen at desks.

One stood and came toward them smiling, thinking they were hot clients, no doubt thanks to the Cadillac they had pulled up in.

Before the poor guy could say anything, Lott and Julia both flashed their badges and asked to see Dewey. The fake smile vanished from the guy's face instantly and he took them down a hallway to the right of the showroom and knocked on a door.

"Come in," a voice said and the salesman indicated they should go in and then he almost ran back to the showroom. Lott smiled at Julia. Sometimes it was fun to mess with people's minds like that.

Dewey Maxwell seemed to be about Lott's age, with a full head of gray hair and a white moustache. He stood from behind his desk when they came in and Lott was surprised he was taller than Lott's six foot height. Dewey had to be a good six-three or more.

He and Julia both introduced themselves, apologized for taking his time, and got him smiling when Julia said the chief wanted them to say hello for him.

"So what can I help you with, Detectives?" Dewey asked.

Julia told him about the case they were working on, then asked about Becky Penn's red Toyota that was sold here. She gave him the exact year and vin number on the car.

"I keep track of every car I ever bought and sold," Dewey said.

"We're interested in who sold it to you and what was the registration on it."

"You saying this car belonged to a girl who died?" Dewey said, shaking his head. "Let me see how the hell I ended up with it."

Dewey turned to his computer and started typing, looking at the note with the vin number Julia had given him.

Lott's heart jumped. Could it really be possible that they would get so lucky as to find out who sold Becky Penn's car?

"Oh, sure," Dewey said, nodding. "Duane sold me that car way back. He has sold me a lot of cars over the years."

"Do you have his full name and records on the car?" Julia asked.

"Oh, sure," Dewey said. "His name is Duane Thorn. Lives down by you folks in Vegas from what I understand. He's a great scout. One of my best."

At that, Dewey punched a button and a printer against the wall started to warm up.

"Scout?" Lott asked, not wanting to trust his guess as to what a car scout did or didn't do?

"All major car dealers use them," Dewey said, standing to go get the information from the printer. "They are licensed by the state to buy and resell cars. They make their living from the difference they can find a car for and clean it up and what I give them."

Lott watched as Dewey took the paper from the printer and then handed it to Julia.

"Here's the information he gave me on the car, the title, and his information and his reseller's license," Dewey said.

Lott glanced at the picture on the license. They guy looked slightly familiar from somewhere.

"He's still around?" Julia asked a fraction of a second before Lott could.

"Sure is," Dewey said, sitting back into his chair with a sigh. "He became a reseller a few years before that Toyota. If memory serves, he had already sold me five or six cars at that point."

"Would it be possible to get the information on all the cars he's sold you over the years?" Lott asked. "It would help a great deal to know before we talk with him."

Lott's gut was twisting and he didn't want to think about what had crossed his mind. They had to clear out the chance that this Duane guy was the guy who killed those four women.

And maybe others.

Dewey shrugged. "Don't see why not. Nothing secret at all about what I do here."

He turned back to his computer.

"Really, really appreciate your time," Julia said. "I'll tell the chief how much you helped us."

Dewey laughed, but didn't turn from his computer. "Never hurts to have the chief of police on your side, I suppose."

Lott glanced at Julia who looked slightly white. She had had the same thought he had just had. She was focusing straight ahead on Dewey, clearly trying to stay calm.

Lott didn't think it was possible that this Duane Thorn could kill for cars, but in the world of killers, Lott had learned a long time ago to never underestimate the evil that some people carried.

TEN

September 17th, 2016
Las Vegas, Nevada

JULIA AND LOTT were back in Las Vegas in time for a late lunch.

Julia found it hard sometimes to understand how fast the rich and powerful could move around when they needed to. But this quick trip to Reno and back had been a clear example of that.

They had sent the list of cars sold to Maxwell by Duane Thorn to Annie and Fleet and their computer people. She and Lott wanted the computer people to see if there was a relationship to other missing persons' cases and the cars sold. She and Lott were hoping there wasn't, but before they went to talk with this Thorn, they needed to know for sure.

Thorn's picture on his reseller's license looked very familiar to Annie, but she couldn't place it. All the way back to Vegas it had been nagging at her.

As they stepped off the plane, Julia actually felt like she was returning home. The air was thinner and much warmer, and all the noise of the airport around her sort of held her like a welcome blanket.

She had lived all those years in Reno, but clearly her home was in Las Vegas.

Lott suggested that they meet Annie and Andor at the Bellagio Café just before two to make sure everyone was on the same page and find out what Andor had discovered about Paul Vaughan's death.

Julia liked that idea a lot. Even with a few snacks on the plane, she was getting hungry. Breakfast had been a pretty good

number of hours before. An entire trip to Reno and back before.

As they left the car at valet parking and went inside the Bellagio, it struck Julia that the Bellagio Café never seemed to change day or night, one of the things Julia loved about it. It was a timeless place and honestly helped keep her balanced in a strange way.

On top of that, the food was good and there was a wide range of choices. There were a lot of great places to eat in Las Vegas, but this one seemed to fit all of them the best.

Annie was already there, as was Andor, sitting in a large booth surrounded by plants and tucked off to the back of the main area of the café. There were no other customers close to them.

Neither looked happy as Julia and Lott approached. Julia had no idea what that meant, but Lott asked what was wrong before either of them sat down.

"Your fear was grounded," Annie said, sliding a paper with a list of names and dates on it toward them across the table. "Every car this Duane Thorn sold to Maxwell was from a missing person's case around Vegas."

Julia just sat there stunned, looking at the list of women's names on the sheet of paper.

"Shit, just shit," Lott said.

Annie sat there feeling sick.

They didn't have four murders. From the looks of this, they had many. A serial killer had been working the Las Vegas area for thirty years and no one had known.

How was that possible?

Could a killer be that good?

"And I have other bad news for you," Andor said.

He slid the copy of Duane Thorn's reseller's license toward them. "Anything look familiar about this guy?"

"Been driving me crazy trying to figure that out since Reno," Lott said.

"Me too," Julia said.

Andor slid another piece of paper toward them, this one with a photo of Paul Vaughan on it.

Julia almost recoiled back in her seat.

They were the same man.

The very same.

PART TWO
Bad Cards

ELEVEN

September 17th, 2016
Las Vegas, Nevada

ALL FOUR of them sat there in silence for a moment until finally Lott decided he needed to get this moving. They had lost over a year when they found the other bodies, and if this guy was still around, and from the looks of it, he was, another woman's life might be in the balance.

"So how did this guy kill himself as Paul Vaughan and still be alive?" Lott asked Andor.

"The supposed Paul Vaughan died from a shotgun blast to the face," Andor said. "Set up to look like suicide. Nothing left to identify, so since the guy was in

Paul Vaughan's apartment, had Vaughan's wallet in his pocket, and was dressed in his clothes, they assumed it was him and that he had killed himself."

Julia took out her notebook and started writing as she talked. "So did this Duane Thorn take Paul Vaughan's picture for his license, or is Paul Vaughan still alive and just faked his death?"

Lott stared at the list and the dates. Three women had disappeared and had their cars sold in the year right before Becky Penn's disappearance. He pointed to the list. "I'm betting those three are the three buried under Becky."

Andor nodded. "We need to visit families of those three, see if we can get anything to identify them from the family that might have been in that grave with the bodies. Clothing, hair length, necklaces, that sort of thing."

"Better than waiting for DNA testing," Lott said.

Julia wrote that down as well.

Annie hadn't said a word so far and Lott knew that meant that something, beside the ugliness that they were uncovering, was really bothering her.

"Daughter?" he said. "You want to tell us what's spinning?"

Annie laughed. "I can't figure out why Paul would date one of his victims, then stage his own death ten years later and write down where he buried four of the women? Just can't seem to come up with a reason for any of that."

Lott sat back and took a deep breath and Julia wrote all that down.

Thankfully, the waitress showed up to take their orders to give him time to think. Annie was right. Not one bit of that made sense.

In fact, killing people for their cars made no sense either. There had to be something much deeper going on here. And with serial killers, something much sicker.

After the waitress left, Andor turned to Annie and Julia. "We know for certain that whoever wrote in that notebook knew where those women were buried and is the killer."

Lott nodded to that.

"But we don't know if it was this Paul Vaughan or Duane Thorn," Annie said. "Or it could have been anyone who planted that notebook.

That made no sense to Lott either. "If you have been getting away with murder for thirty years, why tell the police where four of your victims are ten years later?"

Julia was writing all this down as fast as she could. There was no doubt they had far, far more questions at this point than even theories, let alone answers.

Again, they sat there in silence with the distant sounds of the casino echoing over them before Julia did what she was so good at and organized them.

"So what do we know for certain?" Julia asked.

"We know that all of these are unsolved missing person's cold cases," Andor said, jabbing his finger at the list of names. Lott could tell that list upset Andor. Lott felt the same way.

"We know that a man by the name of Duane Thorn sold all those women's cars to a car dealer in Reno," Julia said, writing.

"We have a physical address for this Duane Thorn," Annie said. "We checked and the address is still valid on his reseller's license and driver's license as of last year."

They sat there for a moment, all thinking. Lott could come up with nothing at all more that they knew for certain at that point. Every other bit of data they had was in question.

"So we give this Duane Thorn's home a drive-by before we send in the youngsters," Andor said.

"No stopping," Julia said.

"No stopping," Lott said. He had no intention of confronting a possible serial killer without major backup. His days of doing that were behind him as far as he was concerned.

"Then, if that's a dead end, we see if we can figure out if that person who killed himself twenty years ago actually was Paul Vaughan," Andor said.

"And how do you suggest we do that?" Lott asked.

Andor shrugged. "Figured we come up with a plan if we needed to."

Everyone laughed and at that point, thankfully, the food came.

TWELVE

September 17th, 2016
Las Vegas, Nevada

JULIA RODE BESIDE Lott in his big white SUV Cadillac as they headed north out of city limits of Las Vegas. Andor had decided he would be better off taking the list of names and getting the files from headquarters.

Annie had gone back to the offices Doc and Fleet kept here in Vegas to keep working with the computer people on various searches. Annie said she would have computer satellite images of the property they were heading toward shortly. Maybe even before they made the thirty-minute trip to the place.

Lott and Julia had promised they wouldn't stop, but just do a recon of the address this Duane Thorn kept. If it actually was a house, the two of them and Andor would present what they had to the chief and more than likely the chief could get a warrant with the information they had about the cars to go in fast and hard.

But Julia had no doubt this all wouldn't end that easily. This killer had been getting away with murder in this town for over thirty years without getting caught or even noticed until the murderer told them where some bodies were.

And even after that nothing had happened for another year-and-a-half. So she had no real hopes this would end easily.

Or that they would find anything at all.

They left the main road about twenty-five minutes north of the last Las Vegas suburb on the two-lane highway headed toward Reno. The paved road they were now on was narrow and wound its way toward Death Valley and other older military sites out in the desert before finally turning back toward Vegas.

After about a mile of mostly desert with a few mailboxes along the pavement indicating dirt roads heading off toward distant houses, Julia said to Lott, "Slow down, should be right up here."

She had been watching the GPS and it showed they were close to the address.

And as she expected, the address was nothing more than a mailbox with a dirt road leading up and through some rocks. The mailbox had the numbers printed clearly on it, but it had seen better days, tilting to one side on its wooden pole. Sand and wind had made the metal look almost gray.

"Call Annie," he said. "See if she has images of that place yet?"

Lott drove on past and then over a slight rise before stopping.

Annie picked up almost instantly. "Nothing at the end of that driveway," Annie said as Julia put her phone on speaker so Lott could hear.

"Nothing at all?"

"Road goes up and makes a small circle around a rock," Annie said. "The road has had some regular traffic but no building. No mine entrance. Nothing."

Julia could tell that Annie was as frustrated as she felt.

"How close in can you get on the ground around that turn-around?" Lott asked. "And can you do any other kind of imaging?"

Annie paused for a moment, then said, "Dad, are you thinking we might have found a burial ground?"

"Exactly what I'm thinking," Lott said. "But damned if I want to go up there to look because, for all we know, it might be monitored or have explosives set."

Julia was impressed. She hadn't thought of any of that. But the moment Lott said it, she knew he might be right. They had dealt with that smart of a criminal in the past.

And if they were going to catch this guy, they couldn't go stumbling into places. They had to assume this guy was really, really smart.

"I'll see what I can have them do," Annie said.

"We're headed back," Lott said.

"Good," Annie said, and hung up.

Julia felt the same way as Lott turned the big Cadillac around and headed back past the target address and toward the main road.

"You really think that might be a burial ground?" she asked.

He shrugged. "If this guy really is killing women and selling their cars, and has been for thirty years, he has to have a safe place to put the bodies. And over that rise looks as private and safe as can be."

Julia nodded. He was exactly right. No one out here would approach any of these houses or go up these driveways without an invitation. Too many survivalist types living out in these rocks.

"So we need to figure out exactly who this Duane Thorn really is," Julia said after they rode in silence for a minute.

Lott nodded. "But what has me puzzled is why tell us about that other grave by planting that journal?"

Julia had no idea on that either.

"What's different about those first four?"

"His first?" Julia said, knowing that was the answer. "Before he got this property?"

Lott glanced at her and smiled.

Julia knew at once she was on to something. She redialed Annie and before Annie could even say hello this time, she asked, "When did this Duane Thorn buy this property out here?"

"Hang on," Annie said.

Lott had reached the main road and turned back toward Las Vegas. Julia felt a sense of relief just being off that road.

Annie came back. "Two months after Becky Penn went missing."

"One explanation down," Lott said, smiling.

"How much did he pay for it? Do you have those records?"

"Twenty acres for nine thousand," Annie said. "He paid cash."

Julia had another idea. "Can you tell me from the list we got in Reno how much Thorn made from selling Becky's car and the three he sold before hers?"

Lott was nodding.

Annie took a moment, then said almost too low for them to hear, "Nine thousand dollars total for all the cars."

"Damn, damn, damn," Julia said softly. "I so wanted to be wrong on that."

"I'll keep working on the satellite images," Annie said and hung up.

"So why did he plant the location in Paul Vaughan's journal, assuming Duane Thorn wasn't Paul Vaughan?"

Julia knew the answer. "To clean up what he considered a loose end," she said. "He expected that journal to be found when Vaughan killed himself, or was murdered, as the case might be. Put all the blame on a dead man and he would be free to move forward."

Lott nodded. "I think you are right."

"I hope I'm not," Julia said. "Because if I am a lot of women have died in all the years since."

"Yeah," Lott said.

They rode the rest of the way back to Las Vegas in silence.

THIRTEEN

September 17th, 2016
Las Vegas, Nevada

IT HAD BEEN a very long day and it was barely five in the afternoon when Lott pulled into his driveway. He and Julia had picked up a large bucket of KFC and it smelled wonderful sitting on the console between them the last mile.

Annie and Andor were both coming over when they broke clear of what they were doing, but as Andor said, he would come by only if there was a promise of chicken.

So they got chicken. And considering that Andor had spent most of the day at headquarters copying old files of missing person's cases, he deserved chicken.

As they went into the kitchen and Julia set the chicken on the table, Lott decided they needed a little something to distract from thinking about the case for a moment.

"Got something I want to show you," he said.

He took her hand and led her through his dining room and toward the bedrooms.

"If you're thinking what I think you are thinking," Julia said, laughing, "you know your daughter might show up at any minute."

Lott laughed. "I was sort of thinking that, but I wanted to show you some remodeling I had done lately."

He took her into what had been the house's master bedroom, but was now a massive double walk-in closet with all built-in cabinets and clothes racks. He had had it all made of a light oak and put in cam lights over each dressing area, with two large mirrors on the walls of each area as well.

He had moved his clothes into one side of the closet and sadly everything he owned didn't begin to fill the space.

"Wow," Julia said, stepping into the room and just stopping. "What did you do with the bed?"

"Annie's old room," he said. "She assured me she would never be using it again."

Julia laughed. "With as much money as she has, not counting Doc's fortunes, I don't think there is any worry of her moving home."

"I left the door to the master bath at the back of this room," Lott said, pointing, "and opened another door into the master bath from Annie's old room, so this entire three rooms becomes one big master suite."

"Wow, just wow," Julia said, walking through the empty part of the closet and into the remodeled bathroom.

Lott was almost as proud of the bathroom remodel as he was of the closet. Designed perfectly for two people with a large vanity with two sinks, a shower, a whirlpool tub and a toilet room that could be closed off.

After she looked into the bedroom area with the new king bed, she turned back to Lott. Lott was very glad to see that she was smiling one of the happiest smiles he had seen on her.

"You interested in saving some money on rent?" he asked, indicating the new closet and bathroom. "This place is all paid off and I also have the third bedroom set up as an office with two computers and work stations."

Julia came toward him and just kissed him, one of the hardest kisses she had ever done.

Then she pushed him back and held him at arm's length. "Carol's things? And are you sure you are ready?"

"I have what I wanted to keep of Carol's things in boxes in the storage area off the poker room downstairs. Tucked away safe and sound."

Julia nodded, but kept looking at him.

"I'm ready," he said. "Carol told me she wanted me to move on after she died. I didn't believe I ever could. But I never believed I would meet a woman like you either."

"I can't replace Carol," Julia said. "And I never want to."

Lott nodded. "I know. What you and I have together is very different than what I had with Carol, just as what you and I

have I imagine is different from what you had with that former husband of yours."

Julia laughed at that because her former husband was in prison at the moment and had married five women at the same time as he had been married to Julia.

"That's why I did all this remodeling of the front room and the layout of the house and these rooms," Lott said. "Not to erase Carol, but to give us a new starting place, since we both love that poker room downstairs so much."

"And that wonderful new kitchen you put in as well," Julia said, smiling.

"So we start fresh?" he asked.

"We start fresh," she said, nodding. "But I'm hiring movers to move everything."

"Oh, thank heavens," Lott said, laughing. "I'm way too old to be doing that."

Then as they were kissing again and Lott was about to pull Julia into the new bedroom, they heard Annie's voice. "Anyone home?"

"Back here," Lott shouted.

"Has she seen this yet?"

Lott shook his head and smiled at Julia.

"Oh, this is going to be fun," Julia said.

And it was as Annie praised the remodeling and then gave both of them a huge hug.

And then she looked into her father's eyes and said, "About damn time, Dad."

And that made it all perfect.

FOURTEEN

September 17th, 2016
Las Vegas, Nevada

JULIA AND LOTT were sitting in the kitchen nook, overlooking the yard, side by side, holding hands. Annie sat across from them and they were talking about everything but the case.

Julia couldn't believe she had just agreed to move in with Lott. And wasn't even the slightest bit scared about it. Clearly Lott was past his deceased wife and Annie loved the fact that they were together. So Carol would not be forgotten, but Julia and Lott could now move forward into a new life together.

In an almost completely remodeled home as well, one that Julia felt very comfortable in.

So finally, with the tub of chicken smelling wonderful between them, they heard Andor's car pull into the driveway.

"I'll go see if he needs help with files," Annie said, standing.

"I'll get the plates and napkins," Julia said, standing.

"Silverware and water," Lott said, standing.

By the time Annie and Andor came in both carrying an armload of files, the table was set and the lid was off the bucket of chicken. And wow did that smell good. Julia had no idea how hungry she had gotten. It had been a very long day so far and from the looks of the piles of files Andor had and a couple small files that Annie had brought, the day was far from over.

All four of them made it through their first piece of chicken in record speed and were working on second pieces when Andor finally brought the conversation around to the case.

"The chief is very interested in what we are doing," Andor said. "I filled him in a little and promised him we'd keep him up to date on everything. To solve this many unsolved cases at once would be a real boost for him."

"And give a lot of closure to a lot of families," Annie said a moment before Julie could say it as well.

Julia didn't like the size of that stack of files, knowing that every file had a missing and most likely dead person that was the subject.

She took out her notebook and opened it.

"So we got answers to a few questions from lunch," she said, looking at her notes. "We know that no one lives at Duane Thorn's address."

"I checked," Annie said. "That is the only property he owns under that name. He only reports his income from selling cars and best as we can figure, his Social Security number is fake. Duane Thorn basically doesn't exist."

All of them nodded. That was no surprise at this point to Julia.

"And we have a theory about why the four women in the other grave," Lott said. He explained the idea they had about why the killer tried to tell people about that grave when Paul Vaughan died, but no one looked at the journal until they found it.

It sounded very logical, but it was only a theory, so on her notes, Julia put down the theory and circled the word "theory."

"So any luck on surveillance of that turnaround area?" Lott asked Annie.

She shook her head. "Can't get anything better than what I have."

Now Available
from all your favorite booksellers
in trade paper and electronic editions.

USA TODAY BESTSELLING AUTHOR

DEAN WESLEY
SMITH

MORNING SONG

A SEEDERS UNIVERSE NOVEL

She quickly passed out high-altitude photos of the turnaround area on Duane Thorn's land. There were a couple acres up there where bodies could be buried in that desert and rock.

Julia stared at the picture for a moment and then felt her stomach twist a little. They really needed to look at that property up close, but if they got a warrant and went charging in there, more than likely it would warn off the murderer. Let him know they were on to him.

"But I have an idea how we could get images we need without being seen," Annie said. "We fly a drone over the place, high enough to not be noticed, but with good enough cameras to get the different forms of images we need."

Julia looked at Annie, who was smiling.

"That's got to be some pretty sophisticated drone," Lott said, looking puzzled at his daughter. "Don't tell me Doc and Fleet just happen to have one."

"Nope," Annie said. "They don't. But we have a team that works with us on different stuff that does. We all are meeting them tomorrow morning at 9 a.m. at the Bellagio Café to explain what we are looking for and what we need."

"And this team can be trusted?" Andor asked.

Annie just laughed. Then she said, "When you meet them, you'll know why I laughed."

FIFTEEN

September 17th, 2016
Las Vegas, Nevada

THEY ALL ATE a second piece of chicken and Andor and Annie both started into their third as they talked, trying to even recognize pieces of a puzzle that they weren't even sure fit together.

Lott didn't much like what they had so far. But at least they had a suspect.

They did know for a fact that a man calling himself Duane Thorn had sold cars of women who had gone missing shortly after their disappearances. How he got those cars no one knew, but the theory was he killed for them.

They knew that Duane Thorn's official address was a mailbox at the head of a dead-end dirt road. The road was used regularly and had a suspicious turnaround at the end that was out of sight of anything around it.

But other than that one license with the state, the picture on the license, and the one piece of property, Duane Thorn did not exist, did not have a history, and seemed to have come into existence about a year before Becky Penn vanished.

They had four bodies in an old grave and four cars, so they were very close to putting together who the other three bodies in the grave were with Becky Penn.

A couple other members of the Cold Poker Gang were running down the families of the missing women to see if they could get identifying information to at least identify the bodies in the grave. And Annie had promised that she and Doc and Fleet could get DNA preliminary testing done within two days if needed.

Beyond that, they had nothing else but theories and questions.

Lott was no longer sure that Paul Vaughan, Becky Penn's boyfriend at the time of her disappearance, actually was dead. And if not, who had had his face blown away with a shotgun?

And they had no idea how that journal got into Paul Vaughan's things, but then was overlooked for decades. Or maybe even his sister planted it. Again, nothing solid, just questions.

But they did have a stack of missing persons' cases sitting on the kitchen counter that they had picked out because of cars sold by Duane Thorn. Every woman in those missing person's cases had a car vanish as well.

So after they were all finished with dinner, they took all the files out into the dining room area and moved all the chairs back from the big table and out of the way. Then starting with the three files from before Becky went missing and going from there in chronological order, they put the files on the table and Annie labeled the top of each with a big sticky note as to the day the woman went missing.

Lott knew they were looking for patterns and it became very clear very quickly that there was a pattern.

A very distinct pattern.

Four women with cars sold by Duane Thorn vanished per year.

And each vanished on the same date every year. The 3rd of March, June, September, and December. And they were all twenty-two years old.

"Three months apart exactly," Annie said softly when Julia pointed out the pattern. "And all the same age."

"Why the exact date?" Andor asked.

Lott watched as Julia wrote that in her notebook as a question.

"And what does he do in the three months between the kidnappings?" Annie asked.

Lott didn't want to say what he was about to say next, but he went ahead.

"The real question is what he does with the women in those three months. Does he kill them instantly or keep them alive for months for some sick reason."

Annie pointed to the last car sold ten days before. "If he keeps the women alive for a month or so, this woman is still alive somewhere."

Annie opened up the file and showed them all the picture of the beautiful blonde college-age girl named Mary May.

Lott stared at her picture and now knew that he wasn't going to sleep much until they ran this bastard to the ground and stopped him.

This was no longer a disappearance case for Mary May. This might be a rescue.

At least he hoped it was.

SIXTEEN

September 18th, 2016
Las Vegas, Nevada

NINE IN THE MORNING in the Bellagio Café felt the same as ten at night. Julia loved that about the place. Time didn't exist there.

She and Lott and Annie and Andor were all there to meet the people with the drone. Annie had told them that they could trust Mike and Heather with their lives and she and Doc had a number of times.

Lott knew them from the first case where Doc and Annie had met. He had told Julia last night before they curled up and fell asleep that he liked them a lot.

Julia was a little surprised when Mike and Heather walked up to their table, though.

Mike Dans was a large, muscular man with a full beard and moustache. He wore a blue button-down shirt, bright Bermuda shorts and tennis shoes. He looked exactly like a tourist.

Heather Voight had medium-length blonde hair and was dressed in a white blouse, jeans, and tennis shoes. She looked to be in stunningly good shape as far as Julia could tell.

Mike was former special forces and his company hired special forces for security still. Heather was a former FBI agent and had been working with Mike for as long as Doc and Annie had been together. They were clearly a couple.

Julia liked both of them at once. They seemed easy going and fun and very competent.

Annie started off giving Mike and Heather the background on the case after they all ordered breakfast. And then she showed the satellite photos she had of the property.

"So basically what you think might be there," Mike said, studying the images and then sliding them to Heather, "is a body dump?"

All of them nodded.

Julia hated thinking of terms like body dumps, but she understood that was the correct way the military thought. And considering that if their worst fears came true, there might be over one hundred bodies in that desert. A body dump by any definition.

"We can't have the person who owns the land even knowing we are in there," Lott said.

Mike nodded. "We'll do a security scan first to see if anything is watching that driveway and road. If there is no surveillance, we can go in there with better equipment and scan the entire area."

"If there is surveillance," Heather said, "we can get a drone in at a thousand feet and take some damn fine images, including ground penetrating work."

"What about Bob?" Mike asked Heather, raising an eyebrow at her.

She thought for a moment and then nodded. "This might be worth his time considering the scope of all this."

She turned to the rest of them to explain. "We both have a good friend who might be able to get some really detailed and ground-penetrating satellite images of that sight. I'll check if we need to."

"Give us this afternoon to check what we are dealing with out there," Mike said, "including the road in and out of the place from the highway."

Julia felt so much better that Mike and Heather were dealing with that property. She just hoped they didn't find a really fresh grave there of a young woman by the name of Mary May.

Julia really wanted Mary May to still be alive.

SEVENTEEN

September 18th, 2016
Las Vegas, Nevada

AFTER THE BREAKFAST meeting, Annie headed back to the office to work on more computer searches to see if she could get any patterns out of all the cases besides the obvious ones of dates and age.

Andor headed to police headquarters to brief the chief on what they were doing and Lott and Julia went to pay a visit to Paul Vaughan's sister. They had talked to her a year before and got the ledger that led to the one grave, but now they had a bunch more to ask her.

They had called her and she had said she would be glad to talk with them again and gave them her new address.

Lott pulled up in front of the suburban home in what looked like an upscale neighborhood. He had no idea how Jennifer Season afforded such a place. Her husband, a card dealer on the strip, had died twenty years before of cancer, fairly close to the same time as Paul had killed himself.

Jennifer and Paul's family had no money that Annie's computer people could find either.

But Lott knew that just the HOA dues on this house had to be high, considering the subdivision. So Lott made a mental note to have Annie really dig into Jennifer's money source. At this point he was grasping for straws. Any straw.

As they climbed out in to the morning air that smelled of mown lawns and wet dirt, Julia said, "Swanky digs."

"My thoughts exactly," Lott said, looking around. The modern street was very silent, all the blinds closed. Everything was perfectly kept up and not even a child's toy remained on the grass. Nothing actually was moving at all and it felt more like a tomb than a neighborhood.

On the way from breakfast, he and Julia had decided they would approach Jennifer with the story that they were trying to clear her brother's name. That the journal had been planted.

Jennifer must have heard them coming because she opened the front door just as they stepped on the front porch.

She was a woman in her fifties, dressed in jeans and a silk blouse. She was trim and slightly muscled. She had on what looked like fur slippers and had her hair up and tied back. She had on a little too much makeup, mostly in a failed attempt to cover some lines under and around her eyes. Lott thought it made her look more like a raccoon.

"Welcome detectives," she said, her voice slightly gravelly, more than likely from too many cigarettes. Lott remembered the last time they had been to her previous home, down off the strip, she had been chain-smoking. This home was a large step up from that house.

She invited them in and offered them something to drink.

Lott and Julia both declined.

She indicated they should sit at her dining room table and they all did.

The inside of the house replicated the outside. Everything in perfect order, best real-wood floors, best furniture, a massive chef's kitchen.

Lott decided he would lead off as they got settled.

"Mrs. Season, we're working on clearing your brother's name on this case with the four dead women."

She seemed honestly surprised at that. "I always knew Paul could have nothing to do with the deaths of those women. He couldn't kill anything and he never wrote a word in a journal in his life. That's why I called you when I found it."

Julia nodded. "That's what we now believe. But we are trying to figure out how that journal got into Paul's things."

Jennifer shook her head. "He lived alone in a house down near the university.

That's where he killed himself and after everything with my husband passing, all I did was pack up Paul's things that were there. The journal was down in the middle of a box of his stuff, so it had to have been in his things when he died. The police at the time never saw it I guess."

Julia wrote in her notebook. They had found that having one of them write stuff down, even though they already knew it, sometimes made a person being interviewed open up, feel more important. Human nature that when your words had enough value to be written down, you wanted to say more.

"Are your parents still alive?" Julia asked.

Jennifer shook her head. "Both died in a car wreck when I was twenty-two and Paul was twenty."

"Oh, I'm sorry to hear that," Julia said.

Jennifer shrugged. "Mother was driving, fell asleep at the wheel on the way back from San Francisco. I was in the car and barely survived. I was in the hospital for a month. It was very traumatic for Paul. For me as well."

"I can imagine," Lott said.

Something was feeling very wrong about all this, but darned if he could put his finger on any of it. His little voice was shouting that they needed to dig a lot deeper into this family than they already had.

And figure out where her money was coming from exactly.

After a few more questions, Lott and Julia stood.

On the way to the door, Julia said, "We'll let you know when we clear Paul's name."

Lott was watching Jennifer's face and just a twitch of a smile hit the corner of her lipstick-covered lips. Then she said, "Thank you, Detectives, for the good work."

As he and Julia climbed back into the Cadillac and he started it, he turned to Julia. "Did you get the sense she was laughing at us?"

"That good work comment," Julia said, "was superstar sarcastic levels."

"So what are we missing?" Lott asked as he headed down the rich, suburban street.

"Everything," Julia said. "Clearly everything."

EIGHTEEN

September 18th, 2016
Las Vegas, Nevada

THEY HAD ONE more interview to do. Annie and her computer people had discovered that old and close friends of Paul and Jennifer's parents were still alive and living in a retirement apartment just off the Strip. Ray and Lorraine Walter.

Lott had called them and asked to talk about the Vaughan family if they had time and the Walters had both agreed.

The retirement apartment complex turned out to be very nice, with large expanses of green lawn and palm trees surrounding what looked like small two-bedroom cottages. The complex had a large function space near a pool and the Walters had wanted to meet there. They were going to watch their two grandkids swim in the pool.

Lott was impressed by the health that radiated from the Walters. Both were clearly in shape and tanned. Lorraine was short, slim, and still seemed to have freckles on her face. She wore a blue sundress and a large blue hat.

Ray stood straight and tall and was about Lott's height, with an easy smile and an attitude that he had survived and from here on out everything was just funny.

They both walked and acted much younger than their mid-seventy years. Lott decided in ten years he wanted to be exactly like them. And he never knew, maybe either Julia's daughter or Annie might end up giving them grandkids.

But to be in that kind of shape in ten years, he was going to need to start joining Julia at the gym regularly. Might be easy once they started living together.

After introductions to the Walters and their eight- and ten-year-old grandkids who headed for the pool at top speed, they all settled around a metal pool table tucked back in the shade beside the brick pool building. The late morning was still cool enough to make the table comfortable and there was just enough of a breeze to keep the air moving around them.

"So what can we do for you, detectives?" Lorraine asked, pulling off her hat and dropping it beside her chair.

"We're looking for any information we can about the Vaughan family," Julia said.

"Messed up," Ray said, shaking his head.

That surprised Lott and clearly Julia had been surprised at that answer as well.

Lorraine laughed and waved off her husband's comment. "They just had some different beliefs than were completely common."

"Walking around in the nude all the time in their backyard is messed up," Ray said. "And letting their kids do it as well after they hit puberty. Messed up."

Lorraine laughed. "They believed in nudity and free love or some such nonsense. We lived next door to them. We could see their backyard from our upstairs windows and we weren't the only ones in the neighborhood who could."

"We saw things we didn't want to see," Ray said, shaking his head in clear disgust.

"Can you mention one or two?" Julia asked. "We really are trying to get a picture of the entire family."

Lorraine glanced at Ray and he shook his head.

"Might as well tell them. Dead can't hurt us now," Ray said.

Lorraine shook her head and Lott could tell she wasn't going to say anything.

Ray, clearly disgusted still after all the years, was far from shutting up.

"Paul and his sister used to have sex out on that patio," Ray said. "When I told their parents, they both laughed and said they knew. That it was natural."

Lott and Julia both sat back. Lott was feeling stunned.

"Messed up," Ray said, shaking his head.

Lorraine waved her husband's comments away. "Why are you interested? Did Paul do something?"

"Paul supposedly killed himself twenty years ago," Julia said. "His sister cleaned up his things. We just talked with her."

Lorraine just looked puzzled and Ray laughed.

"Why was that funny?" Lott asked, feeling more confused than he had in a long time.

"Because both parents and Jennifer were killed in a car wreck over thirty years ago," Lorraine said. "They were coming back from some nudist free-love thing in San Francisco."

"Can you imagine they invited us to go along?" Ray asked, then laughed again. "Damn lucky we didn't swing that way or we might have been in that car."

Lott looked at Julia and she was blinking.

Oh, shit, they had just played right into Paul's hands.

Lott stood and Julia followed almost instantly. He reached out and shook Lorraine's hand. Then Ray's hand.

"Thank you," Lott said. "This information will really help us."

"After it's all over," Ray said, "mind coming back and filling us in on just what the hell is going on?"

Julia laughed. "We will and that's a promise."

At that they both almost ran for the car.

On the way back out to the subdivision where they had met Jennifer, Julia filled in Annie on what they had just discovered.

"He's good," Annie said. "He covered her death in a really amazing way. I'll find out how."

By the time they got back to the expensive house in the subdivision, the For Sale sign was back up and the realtor lock-box was back on the door.

Whoever that Jennifer was had put on a show for them using an empty house. No wonder the house looked staged and clean and perfect. It was staged to sell.

As they sat in front of the house staring at the sign, Annie called.

"The house Jennifer gave you the address to is owned by a bank and is for sale."

"We know," Lott said. "We're sitting in front of it right now."

Beside him Julia shook her head. "We were played."

"And Jennifer wasn't Jennifer," Lott said. "I don't know who that was, but I think we now know why he takes twenty-two year old girls."

"Why?" Annie asked.

"He's turning them into his sister and having sex with them."

Annie just sort of gasped softly.

"Ask her to look up two dates," Julia said. "Jennifer's birthday and the date of the wreck."

Lott relayed that request to Annie and she said holdon.

After a moment she came back. "You are right. Jennifer was born on the 3rd of December. The wreck was on the 27th of February, almost three months later."

Lott nodded to himself, completely numb. "So we have until the 27th of November to find Mary May."

"If we haven't already spooked him," Julia said.

Lott didn't want to think about that.

NINETEEN

September 18th, 2016
Las Vegas, Nevada

THEY WERE BACK into the center of town when Lott's phone rang. He handed it to Julia and pulled over into a Burger King parking lot.

"Detective Lott's secretary," Julia said.

Annie laughed. "Driving, huh?"

"Just pulling over," Julia said.

"Tell dad that Mike and Heather have swept the entire location of Duane Thorn's land and there is no surveillance at all. Nothing within ten miles, actually."

"So what's the plan?" Julia asked. After the meeting with Paul dressed as his dead sister, she still wasn't balanced yet.

"Andor and the chief are getting a warrant to search the grounds and will be out there in under an hour," Annie said. "Mike and Heather are gathering up their equipment and will be there in about that same amount of time."

"We'll meet them there," Julia said.

"I'm staying here and continuing to dig," Annie said. "My computer people are damn angry that the sister's death was hidden from them and they want to know how. I figure the answer to that might help us run this guy to the ground."

"I agree," Julia said and Annie hung up.

Julia had never heard Annie be so focused and determined before. She clearly was angry.

Julia told Lott what his daughter had said and Lott quickly got them off the side of the road and into a parking spot and stopped. They both used the Burger King rest rooms and got some fries and Diet Cokes. They also bought six bottles of water in case no one else going out had thought of that. There was no telling how long they were going to be out on that hilltop.

Julia had suntan lotion in her purse and they both had large hats in the back of the car just for situations like this that they didn't have a lot of time to prepare for. There was no doubt the day was going to be warm, especially out on a rock knoll in the desert.

Thirty-five minutes later, they were pulled off to one side of the road next to the address and the weatherworn mailbox of Duane Thorn. Julia was convinced now that Thorn was Paul. No proof other than the photo on a license, but it made sense that he was.

If anything made sense in this case.

Julia had just gotten off the phone finding out where everyone was located.

"Andor and the chief are five minutes out and Mike and Heather just a minute from here."

Lott nodded. "We wait for the chief and the search warrant."

Julia nodded and looked up the dirt road that twisted around rocks to the top of the ridgeline. She had no desire to go up there now or ever, but she knew they needed to.

They had a suspect who had supposedly killed himself almost twenty years ago, a woman, or a man pretending to be Paul's dead sister, and a man who looked like Paul named Duane Thorn selling the missing women's cars.

They had a lot of theories, but sadly, finding bodies would give them even more clues. But between the cars and the strange nature of this road leading nowhere, they did have enough for a warrant.

Mike and Heather pulled into the driveway and stopped. They were driving a huge Ford Expedition SUV. They climbed out and joined Lott and Julia in the running Cadillac.

"Going to be a warm one up there," Mike said.

Julia and Lott turned around in their seats so they were facing them in the back.

"Good thing Fleet's not here," Heather said, laughing. "He has a phobia against snakes."

"Not fond of them myself," Julia said. In fact, she hated them, but had learned to deal with them when needed. She lived in a desert state. Snakes were a way of life.

"See anything up there?" Lott asked.

Mike shook his head. "We didn't really get that close. Only did scans for any sort of metal or electronics or signals."

Julia glanced around at the mailbox. "Did you check the box there?"

"Only thing in there is some mail," Heather said. "We didn't open it or look at it because we figured the police would want to lift prints from the box."

Julia turned and opened the glove box of the Cadillac and pulled out some thin evidence gloves and pulled them on. "Search warrant will cover the contents of the box and I want to see who he's getting mail from."

All three nodded and she climbed out into the heat and moved to the box. She hoped like hell Mike and Heather were right and this box wasn't rigged to explode.

With a stick she found on the ground near the box, she opened the box and looked in. Four letters and nothing else.

She carefully, without touching any edge of anything, took out the letters and looked at them.

Two were junk mail for credit card offers. A third looked like some sort of accounts letter from Maxwell in Reno.

She put all three back in the box as they were.

The fourth was addressed to this address and postmarked Las Vegas. It had no name or return address, but simply a notation on the envelope.

Attention: Cold Poker Gang Detectives.

She waved for the others to join her and they came quickly.

She felt light-headed and the heat felt far more intense than it should. She didn't want to drop the envelope.

But after everything today and now this, she had no idea what to think anymore.

She held up the envelope, making sure she held it by the corner to not smudge any possible fingerprint.

"Damn it," Lott said, turning and walking away after he saw the envelope.

"Looks like this guy is a ways ahead of us," Mike said, shaking his head.

"A long damn ways," Heather said.

"He's been kidnapping and killing women for thirty years and no one has come close," Julia said, carefully putting the letter back in the box. "This is going to take everything we have to catch this guy."

"Then we throw everything," Mike said, his voice sounding nasty and downright mean.

Julia nodded and turned to see where Lott was.

He was on the phone, pacing beside the car, more than likely telling Annie what they had just found.

He looked furious.

Julia looked at the letters for a moment and then used a stick to once again close the mailbox.

They were being taunted. And laughed at, clearly.

And she hated that.

Hated that with a passion.

And she hated worse the feeling of knowing they had no idea who exactly was doing this.

TWENTY

September 18th, 2016
Outside of Las Vegas, Nevada

AFTER FOUR HOURS in the hot sun, they hadn't found a thing.

Nothing.

Not one body, not one stick of reason why the wide dirt road into this area even existed.

Not one bit of the desert around that turnaround had been disturbed in any way. Ever.

There weren't even more than small animal trails in the sagebrush and dirt.

Lott was feeling more and more frustrated by the moment.

Earlier, when Andor and the chief had arrived, Julia showed them the contents of the mailbox and the two of them had decided to take those contents back to the lab and expedite work to get into that envelope and find out what was in it. And they planned on sending out some techs to dust the mailbox for prints while the four of them searched the turnaround.

Lott had followed Mike up the hill and they parked away from the main flat area over the ridge. Mike and Heather had pulled the equipment and Lott and Julia had taken two of the cameras and started systematically taking pictures of the entire area.

Four hours of work.

Nothing to show for it.

This wasn't a body dump.

Someone, on a regular basis, driving different cars from the looks of the different tire tracks, came up here and drove around the rock and then left.

As the four of them were siting in the air-conditioning of Lott's Cadillac, drinking water, Lott focused on the large rock jutting up in the middle of the turnaround.

None of them were talking, the frustration was that high.

The rock had pretty steep sides and seemed to be flat on top. It was a good ten feet tall and the size of a small shed in width.

If they hadn't been parked so far back, Lott doubted he would have even noticed the rock any more than he noticed any of the piles and mounds of rocks and boulders scattered as far as they could see.

But there was something about the flat top of that boulder that felt off.

He was sitting in the driver's seat and turned back to Mike. "Did you check that rock in the middle of the turnaround?"

Mike nodded. "No electronics, or explosives on it or in it, if that's what you are asking."

Lott could tell that Mike was feeling as frustrated as he was. Four hours in the sun without results could do that to a person.

"Spot me, would you, Mike," Lott asked and climbed out of the car and headed toward the big rock.

Julia looked at him worried, but Lott indicated she just stay in the car and cool off.

Just like he always had someone spot him these days when he got on a ladder, he didn't want to climb a rock without someone behind him if he slipped. He used to bounce when he fell, but somewhere in his mid-fifties, he got the feeling that if he fell, he wouldn't bounce but instead break. And that feeling gave going up ladders and climbing on chairs to change a light bulb entire new senses of caution.

Lott walked along the wide dirt road to the rock. The afternoon heat beat at him and he ignored it. He didn't plan on being out in the heat much longer anyway. It would feel good to get home, take a shower, and just rest watching television in his cool television room. After today he and Julia deserved that kind of night.

He slowly walked on the road that circled the rock, looking for an easy way up.

On the far side, away from the Cadillac where Heather and Julia still sat, he found a way up. Nothing was worn as if anyone else had climbed it, but the ridges in the rock formed a clear series of steps upward.

Once he got up there, getting down might be another matter, but he would deal with that in a moment.

Mike came up behind him. "What are you looking for?"

"Honestly," Lott said, "I don't know. The reason this road exists around this rock, maybe? Maybe a path through the rocks we have missed. Anything, actually."

Mike nodded and Lott turned and started up the rock.

Mike stayed behind him and Lott was surprised he found the climb on the hot stone easy. Even after he had spent hours in the sun.

It took only a moment and he found himself standing on top of the flat area of the tall rock. The flat area was about the size of a king bed. Mike was standing below him, looking up at him and shaking his head.

Right smack in the middle of the rock was a white mailing envelope.

It couldn't have been out in the sun more than a day because it wasn't yellowed or brittle from the heat. It was held in place by a fist-sized rock.

"Mike, get your camera," Lott said. "There's an envelope up here."

"You have got to be kidding me," Mike said.

He started back quickly for the car. Lott glanced up as Julia and Heather climbed out.

"Camera!" Mike shouted to them and then turned and came back to his position below where Lott went up.

Lott got on his hands and knees and studied what he could see of the envelope. It had clearly written on it "Cold Poker Gang Detectives. Enjoy the view."

There didn't seem to be anything inside of it, but Lott sure wasn't going to move that rock and find out. Not without a lot of tech people checking everything first.

As Heather and Julia came running toward the rock, Lott stood and said to everyone. "It's another envelope addressed to the Cold Poker Gang telling us to enjoy the view."

"Shit, shit, shit," Mike said. "Don't move and don't touch that letter!"

At a run Mike headed for his equipment in his car.

Lott took one step back from the letter and watched Mike run along the dirt road.

Another letter taunting them.

What the hell was going on?

Lott turned to Julia, who was standing below the rock looking worried. "Call Andor and find out now what was in that first envelope. And tell them to get a tech out here."

Julia nodded and pulled out her phone. She didn't go back to the car but instead moved into the shade on the side of the rock under him.

Lott made himself take a deep breath of the hot afternoon desert air and really look at the area. He had seen everything in satellite photos and on the ground now for hours.

He knew this area.

But what was he missing?

Mike slammed the door on his SUV and came back toward him, carrying a hand-held scanner. Lott knew it was to look for explosives and electronics and other things, including anything buried under the ground.

The device looked like one of those coin-finder devices that beachcombers used. But this one was a lot more sophisticated. Mike had the strap back over his shoulder.

He had worn that machine and Heather had worn another one searching this entire area. But no ground in this area around the turnaround looked disturbed and they had found nothing.

Nothing.

Their steps in the desert dirt were the only ones. Only the wide dirt road had been traveled on.

Suddenly Lott realized what he was looking at.

The road.

"Mike, there's nothing up here but an envelope," Lott said. "So do me a favor and turn that thing on and point it at the road under your feet."

Mike stopped about twenty steps from the rock where the road split and went around the big rock. He looked puzzled, but did as Lott asked.

After a moment he started forward slowly, shaking his head and watching the instruments on the box machine in his hand. Lott knew that those instruments could almost give Mike a visual image of what was below the surface.

Mike started on the right edge of the road and slowly moved over to the left tire track and the left edge, the entire time shaking his head.

Both Julia and Heather were watching him from the shade.

Finally Mike looked around and finally up at Lott. Even from the distance of being on top of a ten-foot-tall rock, Lott could see the haunted look in Mike's eyes.

"He buried them under the road," Mike said. "Four bodies side-by-side."

Lott looked at the road where it came over the ridge where the two cars were parked and then along and around the rock.

Thirty years of bodies, four per year, were buried under the road.

Lott glanced down at the white envelope and the words, "Enjoy the view."

Now all he could see were women's bodies buried under the entire width of the dirt road for as much as he could see.

This was a view that would haunt his nightmares for the rest of his life. Of that, he had no doubt.

PART THREE
Playing the Hand Dealt

TWENTY-ONE

September 19th, 2016
Outside of Las Vegas, Nevada

THEY MET FOR lunch the following day at the Bellagio Café. Last night Lott and Julia had just gone home after the techs from both the county and Las Vegas arrived up on the road, as well as about a dozen police cars from the county and the city.

There had been nothing in the envelope with their name on it and mailed to the box and nothing in the envelope on the rock and no prints or DNA or anything on them.

Julia had felt almost hollow last night after finding where so many women were buried. It was going to take a massive amount of work to match bodies with missing women over the last thirty years, even with having their car information.

Mike had figured there was a pattern of burial on the road after he and Heather had surveyed the road with their equipment while waiting for the techs from headquarters to show up. So that pattern might help as well.

And Annie and Doc and Fleet had called the chief and volunteered their state-of-the-art lab to help expedite DNA testing where needed.

So after a quick dinner, Julia and Lott had gone to her apartment. Both of them had taken showers and just sat on the couch in her living room and watched mindless television. It felt hollow and a waste of time to Julia, but they both needed to do that. Both to rest and to cool down and to give their minds time to think.

Then this morning, Lott had headed home, soon to be her home as well which made her smile, to change and shower again. She had headed to the gym to try to work some of yesterday out of her system.

Now they were waiting for Annie and Andor to join them for lunch. She felt better, actually. Refreshed and ready to try to tackle all this one more time.

Around them the comforting sounds of the café felt good. The green plants, the sounds of the casino, the wonderful drifting laughter of people not dealing with hundreds of deaths.

That felt good to Julia.

So sitting in silence was fine for the moment.

After a few minutes, she broke the silence. "You think the chief is going to kick us off this case again?"

She knew that Lott had to be worrying about the same thing and not said a thing about it.

"More than likely," Lott said. "He's got a serial killer on his hands and this is going to explode nationally later today or latest tomorrow. He won't want a bunch of old detectives around."

"Even after the cases we have solved for the department in the past?"

Lott shrugged and didn't say what she knew he was thinking. They were retired. They weren't actually in the department.

They sat in silence for the next minute until Andor arrived.

He was sweating, since he had walked from his car in the parking lot through the noon heat.

Julia did what she often did and slid a glass of water toward him and a few extra napkins. A moment later, as Andor was drinking, Annie joined them.

"It's a mess, isn't it?" Lott asked, looking at Andor.

"Headquarters is a beehive," he said. "What you two found out there has buried the entire department under a ton of shit. The chief is working with the county, of course, but none of them have the resources to deal with that many bodies. It's going to take them weeks just to dig the bodies out of the ground, let alone process each one."

"I figured as much," Julia said. "What a mess."

"Heather and Mike met with the chief last night," Annie said, "and Heather contacted some of her people in the FBI and they are coming in to help as well. They are setting up a morgue in a warehouse near headquarters. The chief was very grateful for that."

"I'll bet," Julia said, shaking her head. She couldn't even imagine the scale of death they were dealing with.

"So what are they doing about Mary May?" Lott asked. "Any really fresh bodies out there?"

"Some from earlier in the year, but none since she was taken," Andor said.

Annie nodded. "Mike confirms that from his readings."

"So she might still be out there alive somewhere?" Julia said, feeling slightly relieved. "There is still a hope."

"So that brings me to the next question," Lott said. "Are we off this case?"

"Nope," Andor said, smiling. "When I asked the chief that question, he only laughed and asked if I was kidding. He said he needs all the help he can get and wants us to just keep on going and stay out of the press."

Julia actually felt herself relax.

"Oh, thank heavens," Lott said.

Annie laughed. "Ah, come on, dad. I can't imagine you stopping on a case this size."

Lott and Julia both laughed at that.

"We wouldn't have stopped," Lott said. "But doing it aboveboard helps a ton."

"Got that right," Andor said. "I hate sneaking around that station."

They all laughed and ordered their breakfasts and then Julia gave the signal that they needed to get to work by pulling out her notebook and opening it.

Lott smiled at her and she smiled back. Damn it felt great to be working with the man she loved, even on a case like this one.

"So anyone have any theories on exactly who we are chasing?" Julia asked. "List the suspects."

"Paul Vaughan didn't kill himself," Lott said, "and is playing out a pattern with his long-dead sister."

"Suspect number one," Julia said and wrote that down.

"Suspect number two would be Duane Thorn," Andor said. "Whoever he might be."

"He doesn't exist under that name," Annie said. "Except for the license to sell cars, a driver's license, and the ownership of that land with the bodies."

Julia wrote him down, but put a note by the name that it was fake.

"Maybe an unknown suspect," Lott said. "A person who knows about Paul and his sister. A person who imitated Paul's sister back when we first talked with her and again yesterday. A person using the Thorn alias to sell cars."

Julia wrote that down as number three suspect with a big question mark. To her that one didn't feel right, but they couldn't ignore anything on this.

"Let's talk about the unknown person for a moment," Annie said, leaning forward. "What do we know about him or her if that person is the killer?"

"The suspect knows we are investigating and is ahead of us," Lott said. "And he knows what we and other detectives call our group."

Julia wrote that down, then added, "The suspect knows a lot about Paul Vaughan and his family history, enough to create the fiction of his sister still being alive."

Everyone nodded and she wrote that down as well.

They sat in silence for a moment, the distant sounds of casino filling the air with the sounds of other customers in the café eating and laughing and talking.

Finally Annie said, "I'm going to have our people dig deep into the Vaughan family. Every friend, relative, neighbor that they had. Somewhere back there in the past all this started. And started for a reason."

"And why that one car dealership in Reno?" Lott asked. "Seems like it would have been easier and safer to take the car into LA and sell it."

Julia wrote that down as well.

"Any chance those bodies will give us any help?" Andor asked. "I doubt it, but thought I would see what everyone thought."

Julia shook her head.

Beside her Lott did the same.

"I think they were picked for age and approximate looks," Annie said. "My people have run everything they know about the missing women who had their cars sold in Reno and that's all the similarities that pop. Age and looks."

"Figured as much," Andor said. "So while the youngster detectives deal with the mess we dumped on them, we keep going."

"Exactly," Lott said.

Julia looked at the list of suspects. They needed to keep going. But on what?

And how?

They really had nothing.

TWENTY-TWO

September 19th, 2016
Outside of Las Vegas, Nevada

LOTT HAD BEEN very relieved that they could move forward with this without hiding from the chief. That helped a lot. And he had every intention of staying out of the mess that was now police headquarters.

After lunch, Annie was going back to her offices to work with her computer people around the country. They were going to dig into anything at all in the Vaughan family history. Neighbors, friends, anyone they could find who had an encounter with the Vaughan family.

And Julia had suggested before she left that she have her people dig through the leads the police had marked down in each case to see if there were any repeating patterns in the abductions.

And who was the suspect in each case. They knew in Becky Penn's case, Paul Vaughan was the suspect. Had he been involved with others?

Or had an unknown man been involved with a number of them.

Patterns. With this many victims, patterns over the years might just be what broke the case.

Andor took the task of going to headquarters and staying in the background and listening to anything anyone came up with there, as well as visiting the morgue where the bodies were being taken as they were dug up.

Andor said he was going to need chicken for dinner after five hours of doing that this afternoon and Lott and Julia had promised him chicken.

Lott was glad Andor was doing that. It needed to be done, but it would have driven Lott crazy. Andor had more of the patience to do that and take in pieces and put them together.

Julia and Lott were headed back to talk with Lorraine and Ray Walter to try to dig into the Vaughan's past even more while Annie dug from the computer side. Lott wasn't sure if he really wanted to know more details about the Vaughan family. But they needed them.

Julia said, "You know, there is something really bothering me about those cars of the women."

"What's that?" Lott asked, glancing at her as they turned into the parking lot of the retirement complex. He parked in the same place they had parked yesterday and he left the car running to keep it cool.

Around them no one was moving. Not even a breeze rustled the palm trees. It just looked hot outside the car.

"How did whoever kidnapped the women change the title on the cars so that Maxwell wouldn't notice and would buy them? And so the cars wouldn't pop up on a computer search?"

Lott looked at Julia and all he could do was blink.

How could anyone change a title on a car?

Who could do that? Who would have enough information as to how to even start to do that? And the clear computer skills to pull it off so it couldn't be traced, ever, no matter how many owners the car went through after that.

That question was a lot more important than more background on the Vaughans in his opinion.

"Call the Walters," Lott said, putting the car into reverse. "Apologize and ask them if we can reschedule."

Julia pulled out her phone and dialed, then before anyone could pick up, she asked, "Where are we headed?"

"To talk with Mike," Lott said. "I think you might have hit on something."

"I hope so," Julia said, then focused on talking with Lorraine Walter.

Lott hoped so as well. They needed to find out how a title on a car could be altered without a trace. The killer had done it for over a hundred cars, cars spotlighted in a missing person's case each time.

That was a crazy risk to take, yet the killer clearly thought it wasn't a problem and it hadn't been.

But how could it be done and done well enough to sell it to a reputable car dealership?

And one more question that was bothering the hell out of him since this started.

Why even take the cars of the victims in the first place?

Something was going to need to make sense pretty damned soon. This was driving him crazy.

TWENTY-THREE

September 19th, 2016
Outside of Las Vegas, Nevada

MIKE WAS WORKING on a security install when Julia called him and he said he would be glad to talk with them about titles of cars. He gave her directions to the job site, a new office building downtown off Fremont.

"Pull up out front and I'll come out and we can talk in your car."

Julia gave the directions to Lott and it didn't take them long to get there.

Mike must have just been inside the double glass front door of the five-story building and stepped out as they pulled up and climbed into the back seat.

Lott and Julia both turned so they could see Mike as he slid his large bulk into the middle of the back seat.

"Thanks for talking with us on short notice," Lott said.

"After yesterday," he said, "I want to help any way I can to bring this bastard down. Any news?"

Lott gave him a quick update, including the fact that the Cold Poker Gang was still on the case. Then Lott pointed to Julia for her to continue.

"How hard would it be to change names on a car registration in this state without leaving a trail?" Julia asked.

Mike stared at her for a moment. "The women's cars?"

Julia nodded. "The registration records show they were owned by other people before Duane Thorn supposedly bought them and then resold them to Maxwell. But the car vin numbers stayed the same."

"It would be doable," Mike said, clearly thinking about the process, "but not simple. The person who did it would have to have computer access into the records in the state registration in Carson City. They would also have to be able to access the records and cover their computer tracks easily."

Suddenly Mike stopped and thought, then asked, "When was the last car sold to the dealer?"

"About three weeks ago," Lott said.

Julia was starting to get excited from Mike's reaction.

As she watched, he took out his phone and called a number. "Annie," he said, "I'm here with your father and Julia. Can you get your best computer person to check the registration on that last car sold. Trace back computer tracks on who altered it and do it without leaving a trace."

He nodded and hung up.

"You think it might be possible to trace back the computer tracks of the person who did the changes to the registration of that last car?"

"Very possible," Mike said. "I would do it, but I'm not near my protected computers. But Doc and Annie and Fleet's computer people are sometimes better than I am. Hate to admit that and don't tell them I said that."

Lott and Julia both laughed.

"Thank you," Julia said. "How long will that take?"

At that moment Mike's phone beeped.

"That long," Mike said, smiling.

Now Available
from all your favorite booksellers
in trade paper and electronic editions.

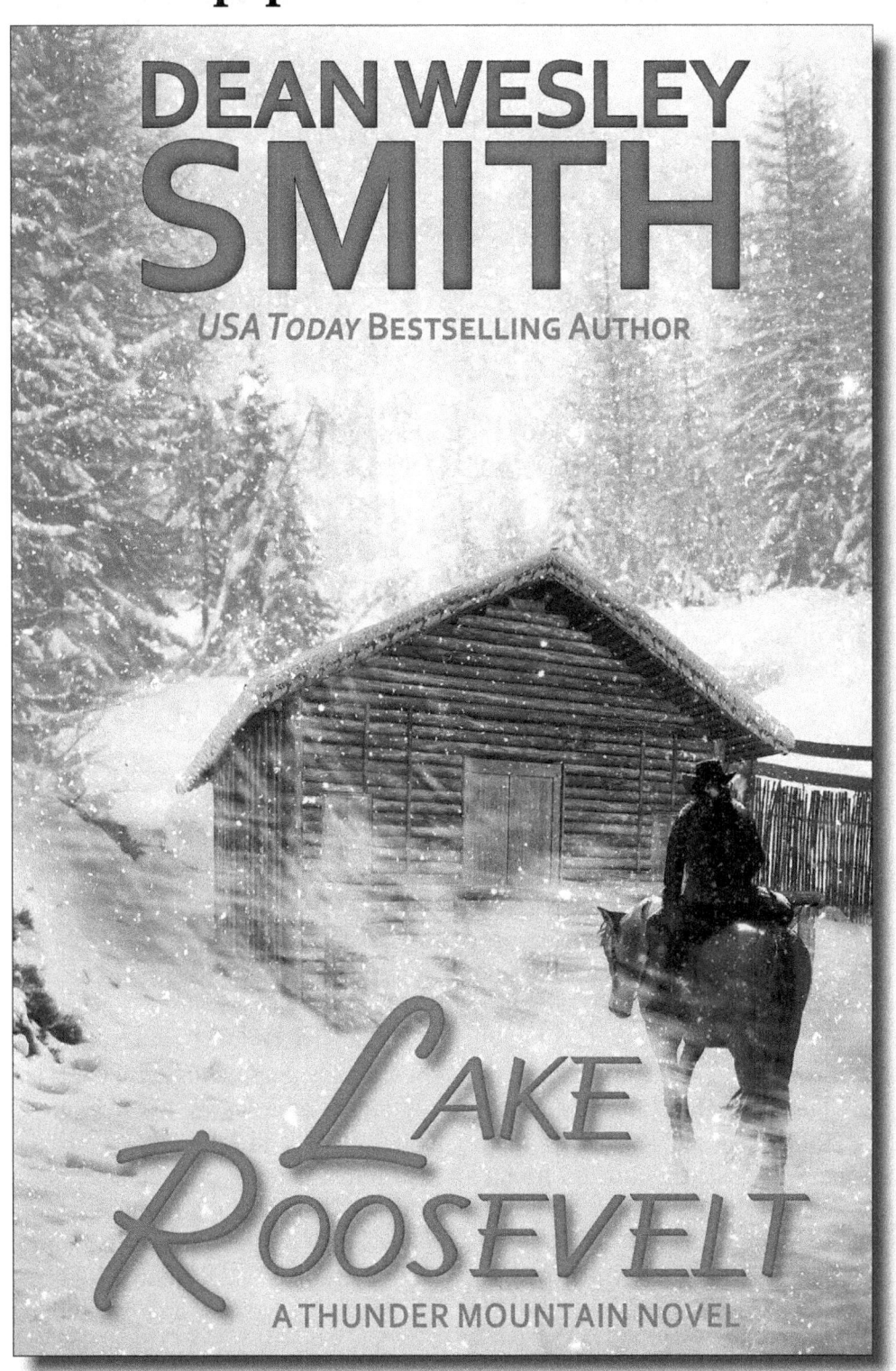

He answered without saying a word. He nodded once, then he said, "You are kidding me?"

He listened for another moment, which seemed like an eternity to Julia as she watched his face take on a look of surprise.

"Go after him carefully," Mike said. "This guy knows what he's doing. I'll tell your father and Julia and they can get researching the guy from other levels."

With that Mike hung up and tucked his phone back into his shirt pocket.

"We're dying up here," Lott said, smiling at Mike.

"Your idea was a great one," Mike said to Julia. "Annie's people tracked the computer trail back without leaving a trail of their own to who changed the title. The guy was good, but not as good as Annie and Doc's people."

"Who?" Julia asked, feeling like a kid in an ice cream shop waiting for the first cone to be passed over the counter.

"Maxwell changed the registration," Mike said.

"The car dealer in Reno?" Lott asked.

Julia was stunned. For some reason Maxwell had never crossed her mind as anything but an honest man.

"One and the same," Mike said. "Your daughter is digging into the guy and finding out everything she can about him without him knowing he's even been looked at. She will report to you tonight at dinner."

Julia just sat there, stunned. No wonder the killer had been ahead of them. They had walked right into his friend's office and told the friend basically what they were doing.

Julia looked back at Mike. "Might want to have Heather tip off the FBI to keep an eye on Maxwell discretely, since

he might be a killer but at least he is trafficking in stolen cars."

"Really good idea," Mike said, nodding. "I'll get that working."

"Thank you," Lott said.

"Yes, thank you," Julia said.

"Keep me posted," Mike said.

A moment later he had slid out of the car and was headed back into the large building.

"So where to next?" Lott asked, glancing at Julia with a smile.

"I'll call the Walters and see if they are still available to talk with us."

Lott nodded. "I'm betting they know Maxwell from back in the Vaughan family day."

"No bet," Julia said.

For the first time, it felt like they had just taken a step forward. Now the key was to not slide backwards. They had a suspect.

But she had a hunch Maxwell wasn't the killer. Finding the killer was going to be even harder, she had no doubt.

TWENTY-FOUR

September 19th, 2016
Outside of Las Vegas, Nevada

TURNED OUT Lorraine and Ray were very happy to help over an early dinner at a nearby buffet. Lott wasn't hungry yet and knew there was KFC in his future in a few hours, but he offered to buy and he and Julia both just sampled a few things off the buffet to be polite.

The buffet and the entire building was decorated in wood and western décor, with saddles and spurs and chaps hanging from the walls and old-looking saloon doors leading into the kitchen area.

The tables were large and made of heavy wood that was polished and covered in a layer of epoxy to stop any stains or glass marks. And everything had western made-up names. Like beef stew was called "Ranch Stew" and so on.

Lott figured every place had to have a gimmick, but this place didn't make him feel comfortable at all, it was so fake.

This early in the afternoon, the restaurant only had about thirty people spread over what looked like ten rooms and an acre of tables. So finding a private corner hadn't been a problem.

"So how is the investigation going?" Ray asked after everyone got seated. "Whatever you are investigating."

Lorraine waved a hand at her husband and Lott laughed. He liked Ray.

"Fine so far," Julia said, taking the lead, something Lott was thankful for. "We are now looking at what might be a friend of the Vaughn family, maybe a friend of Paul."

Lorraine sampled her green Jell-O with some sort of fruit. "What's the name?"

"Maxwell," Lott said.

Lorraine laughed and Ray snorted at that.

"So you knew them?" Lott asked. His heart was racing at the idea that there could be a real link between Maxwell and the Vaughan family.

"Sure," Lorraine said. "They were the neighbors on the other side of the Vaughan house from us. They often joined the Vaughan clan in the back yard."

"No clothes," Ray said, shaking his head. "And the older Maxwell woman should have kept them on, let me tell you."

Lorraine waved her hand at Ray again to indicate Lott and Julia should just ignore his rude comment.

"The son took turns with Paul on the sister right out there in public," Ray said. "A couple times when both families were together, all nude around their pool. Nothing hidden. Just wasn't right."

Lott sort of sat back with that statement.

So the Maxwell that owned the car dealership in Reno had been close to the Vaughan family. He was looking better and better as the killer.

Or least Maxwell was in this up to his eyebrows.

"Do you know what Mr. Maxwell did for a living?" Julia asked.

Lott was impressed. She was staying on topic while he was swirling around the excitement of having the connection between Paul Vaughan and Maxwell.

"Parents owned car dealerships here and in Reno," Lorraine said.

"Parents were killed on the way to some nudist event," Ray said. "Kid inherited the car lots and sold the one here and moved to Reno."

"Was this before or after the Vaughan car wreck?"

Lorraine shrugged. "If I remember right, close to the same time. Within months of each other, actually. Tragic. Just tragic."

Ray nodded. "Yeah, both the houses were for sale at the same time and instead of naked people in the back yard, we ended up with yappy dogs. The dogs were easier on the eye."

Lorraine waved her hand again at Ray and both Julia and Lott laughed.

They talked with Lorraine and Ray for another fifteen minutes and found out nothing more. So Julia and Lott thanked them and headed back out into the heat toward the car.

Neither of them said a word until they were in the car and the air-conditioning was running.

Then Lott looked at Julia, smiling.

And she was smiling as well. They were finally making progress.

"Think Maxwell killed the women?"

Lott shook his head. "I don't think so, but my bet is that he knows who did and exactly where that person is."

Julia nodded. "I agree. And Maxwell tipped off the killer that we were looking for him before we even got back to Vegas."

"Think the killer is Paul Vaughan, still alive?" Lott asked. "I do."

"I do as well," she said. "No proof, but all arrows point to him. And he has Mary May somewhere, staying on his sick schedule."

"So we need to find where a dead man is living and under what name," Lott said.

"And get that poor woman out of there before it's too late," Julia said.

Lott could only nod in agreement to that.

Not a damn thing he could say.

TWENTY-FIVE

September 19th, 2016
Outside of Las Vegas, Nevada

BY THE TIME they got to Lott's house with the KFC bucket between Julia and Lott on the drive there, Annie and her computer people had tracked the movement of Maxwell back two years, day-by-day.

Julia had just finished setting the table and Lott had bottles of water for everyone when Annie pulled up. Julia left the lid on the chicken bucket until Andor got here to keep it all warm.

Annie came into the house with a small file and took a bottle of water from the fridge and dropped into her normal place at the dining room table, downing most of the bottle in two long drinks.

"So," Julia said as she sat down next to Lott. "Maxwell?"

"He's not the killer," Annie said. "He comes down to Vegas for car shows and car auctions and such about eight times a year. He drives himself and he always stays alone at the Golden Nugget downtown. His schedule doesn't seem to alter at all on any trip."

Annie passed them both a sheet of paper from the file. "See if you can spot anything we're missing."

The paper had three days marked on it and appeared to be the schedule for Maxwell while in Las Vegas.

Julia studied it for a moment, trying to find any hole in the man's schedule. Nothing. He did exactly the same thing every time he was here. Almost every hour of every day of his last visit three days after Mary May vanished could be traced by either his credit card or linked security videos.

From the moment he left his room in the Golden Nugget hotel to the moment he got back, Annie and her people had traced him.

"We have the same data on his last trip," Annie said, "and the trip before that. Beyond that the security information has mostly been lost due to time."

"Do the dates correspond with the dates the women are taken and when we think they are killed?" Lott asked.

Julia was surprised at that question and Annie seemed surprised as well.

"They do," Annie said, nodding. "He always comes to Vegas three or four days after the woman is kidnapped and again a week or so before the date of the accident."

"What are you thinking?" Julia asked Lott.

"Lorraine and Ray told us they saw the two boys have sex with Paul's sister together, sometimes in front of the parents."

"Are you kidding me?" Annie asked, shaking her head.

"Not kidding I'm afraid," Lott said. "And they didn't seem to care, from what Lorraine and Ray said, who could see them."

Julia now understood exactly what Lott was driving at. "So you think Maxwell comes down twice for each woman and he and Paul pretend the woman is Paul's sister?"

"Exactly," Lott said. He pointed to the schedule on the paper. "We just have to figure out how he gets out of this schedule and where he goes."

Julia and Annie both nodded. Julia had no desire to think about what those two men did and what the poor women had to go through before being killed.

Lott then turned to Annie. "Any information about exactly what killed Paul's sister?"

Annie shrugged. "Head injuries from the car wreck. She was brain dead from the moment of arrival at the hospital and Paul had to pull life support a month after the wreck to let her die."

"So that's how this all started," Julia said. "Paul, messed up in the head anyway, thinks he killed his sister."

Then Julia had an idea she didn't want to admit she had thought of, but she had to find out. "Any reports of how Paul treated his sister in the hospital that last month?"

Annie shrugged and picked up her phone. A moment later she had instructed someone on the other end to find any reports or complaints or incidents around Paul Vaughan's sister in the hospital.

"We'll find out," Annie said. "It was along time ago, but hospital records tend not to ever get tossed away."

Lott just looked at Julia. She could tell his mind went to where hers had gone. But there was no point in discussing that until they had some proof.

At that moment, Andor came in also carrying a small file.

He went right to the sink and splashed water on his face and then got a bottle of water from the fridge just as Annie had done, even though there was a bottle for him already on the table.

He sat down next to Annie at the kitchen table and as they all dug into the bucket of chicken, they caught him up on what they had discovered since lunch.

"Also," Annie said, glancing at Julia, "thanks to your suggestion, Heather has the FBI all over Maxwell, including tapping his phones and watching his every move without him knowing."

"Perfect," Julia said. She felt better just hearing that.

She turned to Andor who just finished his second piece of chicken and was wiping off his fingers. "Anything coming up from headquarters?"

"Surprisingly," Andor said, "quite a bit. The young guys are doing a pretty damn competent job on this and keeping me in the loop."

"Like what?" Lott asked just before Julia could.

"The bodies are coming out of the ground from the most recent and working backwards," Andor said, "since it's easier to identify a recent body than a thirty-year-old skeleton. And better chance at DNA evidence."

"Smart thinking," Julia said.

"So far they have kept a lid on this, thanks to some favors from the newspapers and local television channels. But that lid will only last until tomorrow night's news."

"Will the chief be ready by then?" Annie asked.

"He has to be," Andor said, laughing. "This will be a shit-storm and the governor has been informed and will be beside the chief as well pledging help."

Julia was very glad she wasn't in their position.

"The teams have ten bodies in the FBI morgue so far," Andor said. "And the similarities of the cases are all coming very clear. All the women were killed by blunt force trauma to the head."

"Like Paul's sister in that automobile accident." Julia said. It was making sense now even more.

"And worse yet," Andor said, "some injuries to the head happened over a month before the fatal last blow."

"Shit," Lott said.

"I'm going to be sick," Annie said.

Julia just stared at her paper plate and the bones of the piece of chicken she had just finished.

"Someone want to fill me in on what that is all about?" Andor asked.

Lott told him how Paul's sister had lasted after the car wreck for a month, completely brain dead, before Paul removed life support.

"These women are filling in for Paul's sister," Annie said, "with Paul and Maxwell, right down to how the women are killed."

"Oh, shit," Andor said.

"That means we don't have until the 27th of November," Julia said, "to find Mary May, but the 27th of October before Paul starts beating on her."

"I don't want this thing to last another day," Lott said.

Annie agreed with that as her phone rang.

She picked it up and listened. Then she said, "Go ahead, I need all the details."

She listened and then thanked whoever she was talking to and clicked off her phone.

Julia had not seen Annie shaken before, but whatever news she had just heard had really bothered her. Annie's face was white and she was staring down at her plate.

"Bad?" Lott asked.

"Bad as we expected," Annie said, taking a deep breath. "For two nights running near the end of Paul's sister's life, Paul and another man were caught with her. They had undressed her and both of them were naked as well."

Julia didn't want to hear any more, but Annie went on.

"Paul told the hospital that it was part of their religious beliefs and promised it wouldn't happen again. A week later, he pulled the life support on his sister."

Silence filled the kitchen and not even the wonderful smell of KFC could cut through the tension and disgust they were all feeling.

TWENTY-SIX

September 19th, 2016
Outside of Las Vegas, Nevada

"SO WHERE IS this killer and how do we run him to ground?" Annie asked.

Lott had no one idea on that question. As far as any of them knew, Paul had killed Mary May and left the country. But Lott actually doubted he would do that. He had been getting away with this for thirty years. And the way he had taunted them up on the property, someone about to run didn't do that.

"I might be able to help a little on that," Andor said.

Andor opened the file he had brought with him. "I got all the information from the files of the last twenty missing women and went through it. Plus part of the gang has been interviewing some of the families of the victims and possible witnesses to the abductions."

"There were witnesses?" Annie asked.

"Not so much up close, but distant, people who heard something, thought they saw something, that sort of thing," Andor said.

"So you found some patterns?" Lott asked. Patterns had helped them run down more cases in the past than clues. Criminals always worked in patterns and from the looks of this case, Paul and Maxwell were both creatures of schedules and patterns.

"Always a dark blue sedan around the scene," Andor said. "No make or model, but new and luxury. One witness thought BMW, two thought Jaguar, a number of others called it a Cadillac-like sedan."

"Any pattern to where they were abducted?" Julia asked.

"Parking lots with cameras that fed to a cloud storage and were out of order," Andor said. "Every damn one of them."

Annie grabbed a pen and wrote down a note. "How much do you want to bet my people can track that computer work that put those cameras out of order back to Maxwell."

"I was hoping you could say that," Andor said, smiling.

Lott looked at Annie as she finished writing. "Paul would have to have the parking lot scouted out ahead of time. See if your people can get the recordings of the parking lots about five days ahead. We can have a few of the gang scan through them. See if we can pinpoint the car model."

"Good idea," she said, continuing to write.

"And also see if the cameras were working when the killer came back to get the woman's car from the lot," Julia said. "Chances are they weren't working since the killer would have to come back quickly for the car, but no way of knowing."

Lott liked that idea and so did Annie.

"There's more," Andor said. "All of the last ten women's families and friends report that the missing woman had met a benefactor of some sort. Two were looking to get funding for starting a business, two were hoping to get into modeling, four wanted to get jobs on the strip."

"Did any of these people see this person?"

"Not a one," Andor said. "But every woman called her Thorn. Usually Mrs. Thorn."

"Her?" Lott asked at the exact same time as Julia.

Andor nodded. "All of them said the benefactor was a her, a woman trying to help other women in starting up careers."

Lott just shook his head.

"Paul pretending to be his sister?" Julia asked.

All Lott could do was nod. It was a theory. Unless there was something major they were missing and there was a woman helping in all this.

Lott glanced at his daughter again. "Some of these women had to have done some research on this benefactor," Lott said.

"Thinking the same thing," Annie said and jotted that down as well.

"She would have to come up rich and valid," Julia said.

"Does Maxwell have the computer skills to set all that up?" Andor asked.

"He's very good," Annie said, nodding. "So yes. Very likely and something my people should be able to find."

Lott knew that was a good lead, but a dead end. "Maxwell would never set something up that would actually lead us to Paul, just in case the cover was broken."

Silence around the table. They all knew he was right.

"Worth looking into anyway," Annie said. "There might be a hint of truth in the fake identity."

Lott agreed with that. Often fake identities were parts of a criminal's real world in some way.

Julia was clearly thinking along the same lines.

"Where did this name Duane Thorn come from?" Julia asked.

"I know the answer to that," Andor said, smiling, but not saying anything.

Lott just stared at his partner until Andor started talking.

"The deepest body under Becky Penn has been identified as a woman by the name of Carrie Thorn. She vanished a year ahead of Becky."

"She was married?" Julia said. "Right?"

Lott looked at her, surprised.

Andor nodded and took out a wedding picture of Carrie Thorn and her husband, D. James Thorn and slid it across the table.

It was dated a few years after Paul's sister died.

And D. James Thorn was, of course, Paul Vaughan.

Lott wasn't surprised at that, but he was surprised at the fact that Paul had married and stayed married to his first victim for almost a year.

"So why the Thorn name?" Annie asked after staring at the picture.

"Paul clearly wanted to honor his great-grandfather on his mother's side. Duane James Thorn," Andor said. "The man founded a major nudist colony in Florida in the 1920s. And wrote a number of books on free love and the expression of love among families."

"Cult leader?" Julia asked.

"From everything I can gather on short notice, yes," Andor said.

"I'll have my people dig into it more," Annie said. "It might give us a hint as to where Paul is living if he is patterning his life after his great-grandfather."

"Good idea," Julia said.

"Yeah, really good," Andor said.

Finally, some of this was making sense to Lott.

Paul must have taken on the beliefs of his great-grandfather, through teachings of his family. And more than likely tried to get his first wife involved. Lott could only imagine that she objected, especially

Now Available
from all your favorite booksellers
in trade paper and electronic editions.

USA TODAY BESTSELLING AUTHOR

DEAN WESLEY
SMITH

AGAINST TIME

A SEEDERS UNIVERSE NOVEL

when Paul wanted her to have sex with him and Maxwell at the same time, like they used to do with Paul's sister.

So Paul must have killed her like his sister had died and that started the entire pattern that took the lives of many women over thirty years.

So they had a solid theory on the why this was all happening and they were pretty sure they knew who the killer was.

Now they needed the where.

Where the hell was Paul Vaughan, aka Duane Thorn, hiding and holding Mary May.

And how could they get to him without spooking him and having him kill Mary May?

Lott had no idea at all where they would find answers to those questions.

PART FOUR
Better Cards Played Poorly

TWENTY-SEVEN

September 26th, 2016
Las Vegas, Nevada

ONE WEEK HAD passed and they were right where they had been. Lott was frustrated, as was everyone. They all felt a ticking clock with the life of Mary May.

They had made such great progress the first day or so, then everything seemed to just shut off. Lott could only imagine how Paul Vaughan was laughing at them and watching them run in circles.

That morning, Lott had spent just walking the wide halls of the Bellagio Casino, trying to get in some exercise and think. Sometimes walking around people who seemed to have no care in the world allowed him to really get focused.

Julia had gone off to the gym and would join him in the café when she got showered and changed.

Andor was going to join them as well after spending a few hours at headquarters trying to dig up any more patterns coming from the bodies or other investigations.

The chief and the governor had promised an early end to this and the national press after a week were still hanging around, but not in such large numbers. There really wasn't a story once you get past the fact that so many women had been abducted and killed over a very long period of time.

Awful, but not much of a sound bite without new information for the press. A couple days was all they could make that last until something else broke.

Annie and her computer people had dug deep into the history and lifestyle of Paul's great-grandfather. The man had lived a fairly normal life in the 1920s, except that he had managed to convince an entire neighborhood to join his nudist and free-sex way of life. They had built tall fences around the neighborhood of ten families and basically lived in peace in a cult-like compound for a decade or more.

And Paul's grandfather's books preached sex as a way to bond families and neighbors together.

Paul's father had also written a few books that were vanity published that preached that having sex after a family member died with the body would bring the live person closer to the deceased and to the next life in general.

Yeah, Paul's father thought incest and necrophilia normal and healthy. Wow, just wow.

It seemed that Paul and Maxwell all bought into this sick family belief completely. And it seemed that the books from Paul's grandfather and his father had been reprinted over the last thirty years. The books were free and no information from any of the accounts putting the books out there was real or traceable.

This morning, the authorities in Reno, along with the FBI, were going to go in and arrest Maxwell. They had gathered enough information to hold him at least on the charge of selling stolen cars.

Finally, after almost an hour of just steady walking, Lott went to a booth in the back of the café and got himself a large glass of water and a cup of coffee. He hadn't come up with anything new, but the walking had made him feel better, calmed the frustration some.

Not completely, but some.

Julia and Annie came in together, Julia smiling and talking. Annie seemed bothered by something. Lott hadn't expected to see Annie at all this morning, so he had a hunch something was wrong.

So when Julia and Annie both slid into the booth with him, he asked Annie right out what was wrong.

"Maxwell wasn't in his office at the car dealership this morning for the raid," Annie said.

"What?" Lott asked. "Did he not go to work or something?"

"No, they watched him go into the dealership, have a few conversations with some salesmen, then go into his office and shut the door. It seems he had planned for this kind of event to happen and somehow knew the FBI and police were coming. He went through a trapdoor in the bottom of a closet in his office a half hour before the raid."

Lott just couldn't believe what he was hearing.

Maxwell and Paul were the two killers in this case, he was sure of that. But he had always assumed that they had Maxwell buttoned up. Now both of them were in the wind.

"They found all his clothes in the tunnel under the dealership that led to a hidden garage," Annie said.

Lott instantly knew what had happened. "The police need to be looking for a woman."

"You're right," Julia said.

"I already told them that," Annie said. "So far nothing. He just vanished. But what is worse is that his wife has vanished as well."

"His wife?" Lott asked.

"We're investigating her background now," Annie said. "But at first glance it comes up that her great-grandmother was a member of the Thorn nudist commune in Florida as well. And her grandmother was born in the compound."

"Oh, good heavens," Julia said. "How far did that sickness spread?"

"Too far," Annie said. "The FBI is now rounding up the two sons of Maxwell. No news yet if they have disappeared or not."

"A giant step backwards," Lott said. "We had two suspects, one under containment and now we have three, maybe more, none contained."

Julia and Annie could only agree.

And the damn clock on Mary May's life just kept ticking away.

TWENTY-EIGHT

September 26th, 2016
Las Vegas, Nevada

AFTER THEY SAT there for a moment, they all ordered lunch and Andor joined them.

Lott and Annie told him about what had happened with Maxwell and his wife and all Andor could do was shake his head.

Julia had just been trying to figure out how Maxwell and his wife both could have vanished in Reno that quickly. It would be fairly easy to button down the roads in and out of Reno. So all she kept coming up with was that they never left Reno.

And the second time she heard herself think that, her stomach sank.

An impossible thought took over. She could remember numbers of missing women's cases almost every week in Reno. Some resolved themselves, others were runaways, but many fit this pattern of women just vanishing in thin air and their cases going cold.

Could these three have also been working in Reno the same way Vaughan was working Las Vegas?

She took a deep breath and said, "I have a horrid thought."

"At this point any thought is better than where we are at," Andor said.

"I don't think so," Julia said. "I'm wondering why Maxwell, in a small town like Reno, with limited exits out of the city, could just vanish like he has done. And as his wife has done. And what that leads me to believe is that they have a place to go there that is off the books."

"Makes sense," Lott said.

Julia took a deep breath and went on. "What happens if these three have been doing the same thing in the Reno area all this time as well as down here?"

Silence.

"And maybe there is a woman involved with Paul as well, not just Paul dressing up as a woman. Four killers," Julia said.

"Maybe more considering the two college kids of Maxwell," Andor said softly.

"And we don't know if Paul and another woman had kids either," Julia said.

More silence.

So Julia took the idea to the last level. "Have men gone missing in the same way?"

Intense silence filled the booth, so intense that it seemed to even push back the sounds of the casino beyond the plants and café customers.

Extreme silence.

"Damn it all to hell," Annie said and took out her phone.

She quickly had someone on the other end looking up relationships between types of cars missing with women and men missing in the Reno area and cars Maxwell had sold. She also had her tech people search for women and men in the Reno area who had gone missing on the same dates as the missing women in Vegas. And then she had them add in a search for missing men, twenty-two years old, in Las Vegas on those same dates.

She wanted them to do a preliminary search first, as fast as they could and get back to her before going deeper.

Julia hoped like hell she was wrong. But if she wasn't, they had just barely scratched the surface of this ugliness.

And a lot more people had died over the years.

TWENTY-NINE

September 26th, 2016
Las Vegas, Nevada

LOTT ACTUALLY MANAGED to eat a little lunch. All of them did. But not a great deal. Not even the comforting sounds of the casino and other diners in the café helped him.

They were all just waiting for Annie's phone to ring.

The conversation over food was on how Doc was doing in a major tournament in Atlanta. Annie had originally planned on going with him, but decided this case was far, far more important. She had managed to talk Doc into going because Fleet would be helping her and all the detectives.

But Lott had no doubt that if this horrid idea that Julia had come up with actually turned out to be true, Doc would be headed back to help as fast as he could get here and nothing Annie could say would stop him. That was just who he was.

Finally, as they had all just finished what little bit of lunch they could get down, Annie's phone rang.

Julia slid Annie a notebook and pen and Annie started writing as fast as she could as someone on the other side just started talking.

Then Annie said simply, "Search all this down and don't miss a name. I'm likely going to need to give this to the FBI and State Police at some point."

She clicked off her phone and stared at her notes for a moment. Then she took a deep breath and Lott could tell his daughter was haunted by the information she had.

"Men have vanished in the same way here and in Reno for the last thirty years on the same dates," Annie said, blurting it out. "And women in Reno as well."

Lott really wished he had not eaten even the little bit of French Dip sandwich he had managed to get down.

"We're talking almost five hundred deaths between the two cities over thirty years," Andor said about as soft as Lott had ever heard him speak.

Annie nodded and said nothing.

"That also means that if we have their pattern figured out correctly," Julia said. "We have not just Mary May still alive out there, but another woman in Reno and two men."

"And the clock is ticking on all four of them," Annie said.

"So what the hell do we do now?" Andor asked, clearly frustrated, more so than Lott had seen his partner in a very long time.

Lott knew exactly what they needed to do. The same thing they had always done when they hit a dead end in a case over the years.

"We start at the beginning," Lott said. "We have missed something. Something that's going to tell us exactly under what rock these sick bastards are hiding."

"And exactly where is the beginning of this mess?" Julia asked.

"Great-Grandfather Thorn," Lott said. "And the compound down in Florida. Everything Paul and Maxwell have been doing now is coming out of that compound in Florida all those years ago. And since Paul used the Duane Thorn name, I'm betting others used names from that period as well."

Everyone around the table nodded and Annie slid back the notebook to Julia to write notes in.

"One sick family tree," Annie said.

"So we first dig back there," Andor said. "Looking for what kind of clues besides names?"

"We need to find three more body dumps," Lott said at the same time as he was thinking about what Annie had said. "Where were the men buried around here? And where were both the women and men buried around Reno?"

Andor nodded.

Silence around the table.

Annie had said *family tree*. Lott knew instantly that was the key to all of this and the key to who they could trust and not trust.

If Maxwell's wife was a descendant of that sick way of life way back, then others might still be around and practicing.

Damn it.

All along they had been looking at this as a lone-wolf serial killer. They had made a natural assumption, but a wrong one.

This was far from a lone wolf.

These were all cult killings.

THIRTY

September 26th, 2016
Las Vegas, Nevada

JULIA WAS SITTING there, staring at the remains of her BLT and wishing she hadn't eaten as much as she had, when beside her Lott suddenly got very excited, almost bouncing on the seat.

He took a deep breath and smiled at Annie. "You hit the key to this mess."

"I did?" Annie said, looking puzzled at how her father was smiling after all this.

Julia had no idea what Lott was even thinking. Or why he was excited.

"We need an extensive family history," Lott said, "or a family tree as you

said, of everyone involved in that nudist compound way back."

Julia just looked at him. She had no idea exactly where this was going.

Lott smiled at Julia and then his daughter.

"I'm not sure I like where you are headed with this," Andor said.

"We thought this was a serial killer who had help," Lott said. "Now we have just discovered there may be three or four involved with this. Right?"

Julia nodded.

Andor just shook his head. Clearly he was following Lott's thinking.

"There may be even more," Lott said.

"Oh, wonderful," Andor said.

Julia agreed. She didn't like the idea of that in the slightest.

"It all stems back from that compound in Florida of Paul's great-grandfather," Lott said.

"You think we have a cult operating here," Andor said.

Lott pointed at Andor and smiled. "Bingo."

Julia just sat there, shaking her head, trying to digest that they might be uncovering an entire cult that kidnapped and killed people regularly. And had been for at least thirty years.

Maybe a lot longer.

"Damn," Andor said, shaking his head. "Just damn."

Annie was already on her phone.

Julia and Lott and Andor turned to listen to her end of the conversation as the sounds from the casino and restaurant seemed to fade away.

"Drop everything," Annie said, "and do this research quick and very hidden. No traces."

She nodded, then said, "I need a complete family tree of everyone that was in the Thorn Compound in Florida. Where they lived, when they died, and if a child or grandchild is still alive, what they do for a living and if they are connected in

any way with any other family member from that compound."

She again nodded.

"Find any of them in this area who own land under any form of the names from that original compound. And in the Reno area," Annie said.

Julia watched as Annie listened.

"Put everyone we've got on this," Annie said. "And have Fleet call me. We're going to need to get Doc back here."

She nodded and said, "Thanks" and hung up.

Then she turned and smiled at her dad. "Finally, something in all this that makes sense. Good idea."

"After Maxwell disappeared so effectively with his wife," Lott said, "and we found all the missing people around Reno, it started to make sense."

Julia just shook her head. "I can see it now, but I never would have made that jump."

And she wouldn't have. Sometimes Lott and his ability to put parts of a large puzzle together just amazed her.

"Annie suggested it," Lott said. "Family tree."

"One really sick tree," Andor said.

Julia could only agree to that.

THIRTY-ONE

September 26th, 2016
Las Vegas, Nevada

LOTT GLANCED AROUND at the other three. The sounds of the casino around them only a distant background noise. Their meals mostly half-eaten still on the table.

"So what do we do next? Do we get the FBI and the chief and State Police in on what we are thinking?"

"Someone tipped off Maxwell this morning about his arrest," Julia said. "For the moment I think we're better running this down until we have some real evidence and need help. And we might be able to find other members of this cult who would tip off Maxwell or Paul."

"Agreed," Andor said. Then he glanced at Annie. "Can any of your people figure out who tipped off Maxwell either last night or this morning?"

"I have my people jamming on the family trees," Annie said. "But how about I call Mike and Heather and see if they can track that? We can trust them as well."

Lott liked that idea, so Annie called Mike and got him started on that, telling him in quick order what they were thinking about a cult in play on all of this.

When she hung up she smiled. "Mike and his people are dropping everything and focusing on this as well."

"We have an army of skilled computer people digging," Andor said, laughing.

"All the better to dig out the killers," Lott said, also smiling. And he meant that. So many cases in his early years had gone cold simply because they didn't have the ability to dig into backgrounds of people and the time to do some basic footwork. With this many skilled computer people at the tasks, something was bound to break.

"It's going to take a few hours before my people can get it all and we can cross-reference between what Mike finds," Annie said.

"And I need to check in at headquarters and the morgue," Andor said, "to see if anything is developing there."

"So I'll call when I have enough information on families that we can sort it all," Annie said, standing.

Andor stood as well.

"At the house," Lott said. "We can sort it all on the big dining room table."

"Can you get some whiteboards as well?" Annie asked. "Got a hunch with this much data, they will make it easier to trace family."

Lott nodded. He liked that suggestion as well. It would allow them to all see larger pictures.

A moment later he was sitting there alone in the big booth with Julia.

He turned to look at her and smiled. "Looks like we have kicked over a few dozen beehives."

"Did I ever tell you that cults scare me to death," Julia said.

"History?" he asked. He had never heard her mention anything about a cult in her past.

"Nope," she said. "Just that they often have fingers in everything. I'm not sure if I really want to find out who in Reno is part of all this."

Lott nodded. He understood exactly where she was coming from. Reno was a small town and someone inside the law had warned Maxwell. Chances are she was going to know that person.

He took her hand and they sat there for a moment just letting the calming sounds of the restaurant and casino wash around them. They both really loved it here in this restaurant.

Finally he leaned over and kissed her. "Let's leave your car and take mine and go shopping."

Two hours later they had five whiteboards on easels set up around his dining room and everything out of the way.

And still no phone call.

So he led her by the hand and they went into the new bedroom and lay down in each other's arms and tried to just rest.

He had a hunch that it might be the last real rest they got before this was finished.

PART FIVE
Playing the Hand for Information

THIRTY-TWO

September 26th, 2016
Las Vegas, Nevada

THEY BOTH ACTUALLY dozed for an hour before Annie called. Julia felt groggy, but she knew in a few minutes she would be fine.

Annie was on the way, so Lott called Andor and told him that as well.

Julia beat Lott into the kitchen and fixed them both a snack of cold chicken and some corn left from an earlier bucket of KFC.

They both had a cup of coffee to help wake up and by the time Andor came through the door, sweating, it was four in the afternoon. But Julia felt almost alert.

Andor took a couple pieces of cold chicken as well and a bottle of water and joined them.

"Anything?" Lott asked before Julia could.

"They are just slogging away, trying to make sense of years of killings," Andor said. "I can't imagine if we were still on the force and caught something that big."

"We wouldn't have slept," Lott said.

"None of the detectives are," Andor said. "Frustration is high and the chief is getting pressure from about a hundred directions to solve this. They have an entire staff of people set up in some empty offices near the morgue warehouse just dealing with hundreds of families trying to find out if their missing kid is part of all this."

"That's just ugly," Julia said. The entire idea of families with missing girls suddenly being tossed into this just made her shudder.

"If what we think has happened actually did," Andor said, "this will get far, far uglier."

Julia could not argue with that in the slightest.

A moment later Annie came in carrying a large pile of file folders. She dropped them on the counter, took a bottle of water and some cold chicken out of the fridge and sat with them at the dining room table.

"Mike's still working on tracing who tipped off Maxwell and will call when he has the name," Annie said.

"Doc on his way back?" Lott asked.

"In the air as we speak," she said. "It will be damned good to have him back and his perspective on all this as well."

Julia could only agree to that. Doc, like Lott, had a way of seeing pieces of a human puzzle and understanding how they fit.

"Any surprises?" Lott asked, pointing to the folders.

"Honestly haven't looked at them in the slightest," Julia said. "Figured it would be better if we all did that together to make sure one assumption doesn't send us down a wrong road."

Julia nodded. "Good idea."

"Good discipline," Lott said. "Worthy of a major poker player."

Annie laughed. "Actually I never had time to look, or I might have."

"Ahh, the truth," Andor said.

At that they all stood, tossed away napkins and paper plates and headed for the dining room.

Julia took the files from Annie and looked at the names on them. Annie's people had divided all the folders by the ten families in the original compound.

So Julia took the top one, the one that said Thorn Family on it and opened it.

It seemed the Thorn family had some branches over the decades, but by the time Paul and his sister were born, they were the only two of that new generation.

"Names," Julia said. "We need to mark down names and what family they are from."

She went to one whiteboard they had set up and labeled it names and put Thorn in big letters. Annie quickly read her all the names, first, last, and middle, that were attached to the Thorn family through the generations. There were twenty.

Maxwell was the next file.

They did the same thing.

That filled one board and Julia moved to a second board and wrote smaller for the other eight files.

As she and Annie were doing that, Lott and Andor had pulled up chairs to the dining room table and were going through each file slowly, trying to spot any cross-connections among the families.

So finally that name pass was done. Now what?

Julia looked at the three boards full of names and just shook her head. It seemed impossible.

Annie's computer people had also put where the modern relatives were living. So as Lott and Andor kept studying the files for something that seemed likely or out of place or connected, Julia and Annie started sorting for names that were still alive and in Nevada, underlining them.

In the third file of a family that seemed to have been a direct neighbor of the Thorns in the compound in Florida, Julia sort of jerked back and almost dropped the file.

"What?" Annie asked.

Lott looked up at Julia with a worried frown.

Julia moved over to the second board and pointed to the name Walters.

Then she ran her hand down the board until she came to the name Raymond.

"God damn," Lott said, jerking to his feet. "I'm getting damned tired of being played by these people."

"Are you saying that Ray and Lorraine are part of all this?" Andor asked.

"Looks that way," Julia said, dropping into a chair and closing her eyes. She felt about as tired as she had ever felt.

"And who knows," Lott said, clearly angry, "those grandkids they were watching might have been Paul's kids."

"Likely," Annie said, studying the Walters file in front of her. "It says here that Ray and Lorraine had no children."

"And we never saw where they actually lived," Julia said. "Once at a pool, once in a restaurant. We trusted them and they seemed like a nice retired couple and they played us like we were beginners."

"For all we know," Andor said, "they are the leaders of all this, the senior family members."

Julia just sighed. She just didn't misread a person that badly that often.

"Maxwell played us as well," Lott said, " and that woman in that house pretending to be Paul's sister played us."

"What the hell are we dealing with here?" Andor asked, shaking his head.

Julia was asking herself that same question.

THIRTY-THREE

September 26th, 2016
Las Vegas, Nevada

LOTT FORCED HIMSELF up and around to stare at all the names on the whiteboards set up in his dining room. It seemed like a massive number of people, but it actually wasn't that many.

"We need to make sure that none of these people are on a police force or in any branch of government that will have access to what is happening."

"Agreed," Andor said, coming around and staring at the board as well.

Suddenly one name sort of leaped off the board at Lott. It was buried down in the McCarthy family list of names.

He turned and quickly opened the file and his heart sort of stopped when he saw the name, the location of the person, and what that person did. Julia was going to be destroyed by this, completely destroyed.

Lott turned around and said, "I know who Mike's going to find in his search for the tipster."

Everyone turned their attention from the boards and looked at him. He handed the file to Julia and pointed down the list in the McCarthy family history.

Her face went white when she saw the name Norbert. Her old boss. The Chief of Police in Reno.

She handed the file to Julia who took one look and swore and handed the file to Andor.

"Are you kidding me?" Andor asked.

Lott couldn't remember the last time he felt this angry and this used by criminals.

No more.

This blindly moving around and trusting everyone had to end. He and Julia and Andor had made a bad assumption right from the start. They had assumed this was one person doing the killings. That assumption, without question, had already caused them so many missteps and twisted information, they didn't know what was real and what wasn't anymore.

"We can no longer trust anyone on this outside of our tight group," Lott said, going over and touching Julia on the shoulder gently. "Until we have made sure they are not on any of these family lists."

Julia nodded.

"We need a lot more information," Annie said. "A lot more computer searches without being noticed. We need every resource Doc and Fleet can dig up that they trust, and everything Mike and Heather have in their arsenal firing at this. We vet everyone completely."

"We never again underestimate these people," Lott said, the anger just below the surface.

Everyone nodded.

He knew they were all as angry as he felt.

Then he turned to Annie. "Can you have Mike come over and sweep this place for any kind of listening devices? And set up secure phones for us as well."

"Oh, shit," Andor said. "You think?"

"These people may have been killing people for almost a century and getting away with it," Lott said. "And they have played us like we are beginning poker players with large stacks of chips. No more. Time we turn the tables on them. I want a safe place we can talk and plan."

"Exactly," Annie said. She quickly called Mike, told him what to bring and got him on the way.

Lott moved over and hugged Julia, who hugged him back.

She felt almost like a rag doll in his arms.

"The chief might not have had anything to do with this," he said.

She shook her head. "He's in up to his ears. I remember he often told us missing persons' cases were not as important as murder cases. He sometimes moved us away from these very cases. None of us ever questioned him."

"I'm sorry," Lott said. "I know how much you liked him."

"Right now," she said, "I just want to put a bullet in both his arms and then kick him in the balls a few times."

"Oh, that would hurt," Andor said.

Lott hugged her. "Let's see if we can give you the chance to do just that."

"Only if I get to watch," Andor said.

All of them laughed.

And then went back to work.

THIRTY-FOUR

September 26th, 2016
Las Vegas, Nevada

MIKE SAID THE house was clear after a half hour and then he set up a signal-blocking device so that no one could listen to anything said in the house. Then he set up clean phones for all of them.

That made Julia feel a little better. Not much, but a little. She just kept remembering times that her chief in Reno steered her and her partner in a certain direction off of a missing person's case.

She felt sick to her stomach with a deep anger she had no idea if she could ever get past. She had trusted him and he had betrayed her.

When Mike was done, he glanced at everyone going over the files on the big dining room table. "You want to tell me exactly what all this is about?"

"These names are all family members and descendants of a hidden cult from almost a hundred years ago," Annie said, pointing at the boards and then the files on the tables.

"We're starting to get the idea that this cult has very deep roots in both Reno and Las Vegas," Lott said.

"You found the person who tipped off Maxwell in Reno yet?" Julia asked.

"Getting closer," Mike said.

Julia pushed back from the table, standing and going over to one board. She pointed to Norbert's name. "Look familiar?"

Mike shook his head.

"My old boss, the Reno Chief of Police."

"Oh, shit," Mike said.

Julia watched as his eyes got wide as he suddenly realized just what they were dealing with.

"The older couple that we interviewed because they had been neighbors back when Paul grew up?" Lott said.

"Don't tell me," Mike said.

Lott nodded and pointed to the top family name on one of the boards.

"We don't know what's true and what isn't at this point," Annie said. "I have two people searching for any records of that cult that started all this in Florida past the names of the families."

"How did the cult end?" Mike asked.

"We're pretty convinced it didn't," Lott said. "But we don't know anything about it other than from what two cult members told us, and we sure can't trust that."

"We tried to trace the number I got and had called them on," Julia said. "It was a burner phone now off and more than likely tossed."

That simple fact that those two old people had played her made her almost as angry as her old boss being a part of this.

"You got more people you can trust and who are fantastic on computers?" Annie asked.

"I got four," Mike said, nodding. "And Heather and I will dig in as well."

"Thanks," Annie said. "I'll have my people send you all this when you get back and say you are ready. We need help tracking property owned by these people or by names of these people who are dead. Somewhere in Reno and in Las Vegas, four people are being held. And who knows what these creeps are doing to them."

Mike nodded and headed for the door.

"Thanks, Mike," Annie said.

"Thank me when we run these people to the ground," Mike said as he headed into the kitchen to go out the back door.

Julia felt a ton better with Mike and Heather and his team on board this as well.

Twenty minutes later it was Lott who made another breakthrough.

"I think I found Paul's real wife," he said, sitting back, staring at the files in front of him.

Julia stood and went over and put her hand on his shoulder.

"Maxwell is married to Tammy Craig, a descendant of the original Craig family."

Julia moved away and put Paul's name on one of the two blank boards they had left. Then beside Paul's name she wrote Maxwell. And then with a line she added in Tammy Craig.

"Tammy had a twin sister named Wendy Craig," Lott said. "She's a real estate agent."

"The woman we talked to at the house?" Julia asked before marking Wendy Craig's name up on the board and putting a question mark between her and Paul.

"I'll have my people pull up her license picture and her address and have them check it all and send it over," Annie said, grabbing her phone.

After ten more minutes of work, Annie's phone rang and she held up a picture of Wendy Craig, now married and living under the name Wendy Walter."

Annie showed it to Lott and then Julia.

All Julia could do was stare. It wasn't the same woman. Not even close.

So some other woman had been in that house. But who?

"Information coming in about her husband," Annie said. And then she laughed. "One guess as to his first name?"

"Paul." All three of them said the name at the same time.

Julia, for the first time in an hour, felt slightly better.

THIRTY-FIVE

September 26th, 2016
Las Vegas, Nevada

THEY WERE SLOWLY gathering more and more information and making connections. Chief Norbert's wife was a descendant of one of the cult families as well. Lott liked how that felt, but it also twisted his stomach.

This cult was still so buried and so widespread that if the police didn't round up every cult member at the same time with real evidence to hold them, they would all just be lost once again and go underground.

And that meant more innocent people would die down the road in some other city when the cult surfaced again.

He looked up at Julia who was standing in front of one of the whiteboards staring at it, then at his old partner Andor, who was reading one of the pages of family information.

"We need to get our chief in on this pretty soon," Lott said.

"Can we trust him?" Annie asked.

Lott didn't know the answer to that, but he glanced at Annie who nodded. "I'll have my people run a background check on him and his wife. Make sure he's not connected to any part of this mess."

She took her phone and hit a button and walked into the kitchen to talk.

"I'll head there now," Andor said, glancing at his watch. "I'll wait for the all-clear from Annie and invite him to chicken dinner, which I assume will be waiting for us when we get here."

"Count me out on that," Annie said, coming back in from the kitchen. "Fleet is in town from Boise and Doc is landing in forty minutes. I want to get them up to speed completely and working on this from our offices."

"How long on the background on the chief?" Andor asked.

"Twenty minutes," Annie said. "I'll call you."

"And if he's in this mess?" Julia asked.

Andor shrugged. "I'll come back and eat chicken with you two."

With that he turned and headed out the back through the kitchen.

Annie went with him.

Lott glanced at Julia. "Seems we have been given dinner duty. We need a break anyway."

She nodded and headed for the bathroom. "Let me splash some water on my face and I'll be ready."

Lott turned and stared at the boards. In ten original families, there were over one hundred and sixty people still alive. Twenty were children under ten. Almost all of them were living in the Reno and Las Vegas areas that they could tell.

So that left one hundred and forty people that they knew of possibly involved with regular kidnappings and murders. He was having a very hard time imaging that every one of them were involved. Yet most of the marriages they had tracked so far had been among the families.

Religious tight.

But if Thorn had been the leader back in Florida, who led them now? Was this a seniority thing or a bloodline thing? If bloodline, then Paul was the head of everything, since he was the only adult direct descendant left of the original founder.

They needed so much more information about the original cult, the original ten families than they had.

And how did murder play into this? What was it about the age twenty-two? And those two dates. And on and on.

Answers needed to start piling up faster than questions or those four people were going to die. If they weren't already mostly dead.

Julia came out of the bathroom, her face flushed from cold water and her wonderful brown hair combed. She kissed him and pulled him toward the kitchen.

"We have the best computer people on the planet digging for information," Julia said. "We need to get some food and take a break so we are ready to act on the information they feed us."

It took them twenty minutes to get to KFC and get the chicken, and when he pulled back into his driveway, there was a black sedan parked out front on the street, empty.

He had a really bad feeling about this. Really bad.

He indicated the car and she nodded, opening the glove box and digging out his gun and handing it to him.

He took the gun and she took the chicken. There was another gun hidden just inside the back door and she would go for it after he went in first.

They went in silently.

It had been a while since either of them had had to do this sort of thing and Lott could feel his heart pounding. He made himself breathe regularly.

He never expected to be entering his own house like this.

The kitchen was empty, so Julia quietly slid the bucket of chicken onto the counter and then got the second gun.

When she was ready, she nodded to him.

Lott eased toward the door to the dining room. It took him only a second to see one man staring at their boards, his back to them. He was dressed in tan slacks and a tan short-sleeved shirt. His hair was gray and thinning in the back.

Lott studied as much of the room as he could, then indicated to Julia one person and that he would go right.

Julia nodded.

Lott eased into the room, sliding right out of Julia's way.

The man hadn't heard them. He just kept staring at their boards.

"Hands up," Lott said. "And don't even think of moving."

"I wouldn't dream of it, Detective," the man said, turning slowly while holding his hands over his head. "I am unarmed."

Julia came in behind Lott and moved to the left, checking out the rest of the room.

She indicated she would check the back bedrooms and Lott nodded.

She vanished, moving silently as Lott stared at the man in front of him. It took Lott a moment to recognize exactly who was standing in his dining room.

At that point Julia came back, gun still up, and indicated all clear.

"So," Lott said to the man. "What do we call you? Paul Vaughan or Duane Thorn?"

THIRTY-SIX

September 26th, 2016
Las Vegas, Nevada

WHEN JULIA RECOGNIZED who Lott was pointing his gun at, she about had a heart attack. Her breath caught and her heart was beating so fast, she was afraid everyone could hear it.

She let her years of training take over and that calmed her nerves some. After she checked the back rooms, which also gave her a moment to calm down some, she came out and indicated to Lott that she would keep the guy covered while Lott patted him down.

"I am unarmed," the man said as Lott did a complete job of making sure that was the case. "And I go by Paul. Paul Walter to be exact."

Lott pulled a chair out so that it was in an open area in front of the boards and indicated Paul should sit.

Julia still couldn't imagine why Paul would come to Lott's house and let himself be captured. Actually he clearly wanted to be captured even though no one had officially charged him with anything yet.

"So what exactly are you doing here?" Lott asked, moving back and putting his gun away in his belt.

Julia put the gun she had been carrying on the table in front of her and sat down so she could see Paul.

Paul smiled. "I thought I could help with all this."

Paul waved his right had at the boards and then the table. "I will admit, you are making some good progress."

"If you are looking for some sort of deal in these serial killings," Lott said, "I doubt you will get it."

"I have killed no one," Paul said, his voice low and mean. "Can't imagine it, to be honest."

"So who is doing the killings if you and Maxwell and the rest of these families are not doing the killings?" Lott asked.

"And what happened to Becky?" Julia said, barely managing to keep the anger out of his voice.

Paul actually looked upset at that question, which made Julia feel better. Anything she could do to make this killer feel distress would make her happy.

"Becky was killed because of me," Paul said. "I had fallen in love with her and we were talking about getting married. She was outside the families. I thought I had escaped the families by that point. I should have known better."

"I seem to remember you married once before?" Lott asked.

Paul nodded. "Also outside the families. She vanished right after we were divorced and it wasn't until you found Becky's body and the other three that I knew what happened to her as well."

"So if you don't do all these killings, or take part in them, who does?"

"Lorraine and Ray Walter are the head of the families now," Paul said, pointing to the board.

Julia was just shaking her head at that. "They are your wife's parents, correct?"

"You have that correct," Paul said. "But my wife has wanted nothing to do with the families either. We have remained out of their sight and done nothing to antagonize them. And we had no kids, so we are now worthless to them."

"Yeah, we talked with them," Lott said. "Not a lot nice to say about you."

"I'll bet," Paul said, shaking his head. "I discovered they killed my parents and Maxwell's parents to take over the families from my dad. They have always hated that I wanted nothing to do with any of them. They could have used me as the last remaining Thorn to keep others in line if I had just gone along. Now they do it with threats and killing."

Julia just shook her head and clearly Lott was feeling almost as disgusted.

"So before this goes any farther," Julia said. "You want to tell us exactly what this commune or cult your family started is all about?"

"Sex, death, and sacrifices to the Great One, whoever or whatever that might be."

Paul put air quotes around "Great One."

"It's a religion?" Lott asked.

"A real twisted and sick one, yes," Paul said, nodding. "It started out of the New England area back before 1900 and had a lot of followers. My great-grandfather convinced ten families to move to Florida where it was warm and they wouldn't be known. The story goes that the pressure was getting pretty intense on them in New England."

Julia just shook her head.

"Up in the New England area," Paul said, "there have always been rumors about Mu Death Cults that followed the supposed teachings from the lost continent of Mu. My great-grandfather took that idea, added open sex and nudity to it, and founded what he called The Families."

"Those ten?" Lott asked, pointing to the board.

Paul nodded.

"Any new families been added?" Julia asked, trying to ignore the craziness of worshiping a god from a fake lost continent. And killing people by doing so.

"None," Paul said. "It's like a sacred bloodline, which is why my not participating has made them all so angry. Lorraine and Ray killed my parents and my sister thinking they could control me and that I would have kids and they discovered they were wrong."

Lott looked over at Julia and she sort of shrugged. She had no idea what to think. But it didn't matter. He was here now and they could check detail by detail everything he said.

"So one more question before we go back to the start and work through all this," Lott said.

"I'm in your custody until this is finished," Paul said. "My wife and I agreed I should come here after you found one of the family's burial sites. We both knew the family had set me up as the fall guy. She has disappeared and will not surface until I call her and tell her this is finally over."

Julia nodded to that. She had seen that pattern in others turning themselves in against a dangerous situation.

"Do you know where they are keeping the four they have kidnapped recently?" Lott asked.

"I think I do," Paul said. "I have never been to either the place here or in Reno. They are called Family Gatherings. But I think I can give you enough information to find the property. And enough to find the other grave sites and give those pour souls closure."

Julia just sat back, stunned. This almost felt too good to be true, so more than likely it was another bad road. But at this point it was their only road.

Lott just shook his head and at that moment both Andor and the chief appeared in the kitchen door, guns drawn.

The chief was a tall, wide-shouldered man with silver hair who tonight had on a dress shirt and black slacks, but had clearly lost the coat and tie somewhere along the way here.

"Wow, you two are quiet," Lott said, looking around at them surprised.

"Tough to be with that chicken smelling so good in the kitchen," Andor said. "It was a toss-up between your life and a chicken leg."

"I voted for the chicken leg," the chief said.

Julia smiled. Clearly Annie's research had given the chief the all clear.

Then she looked at Paul. If even a part of what he had been saying was true, then once again they had been on the wrong path, making bad assumptions.

Assuming that he was the killer. He still might be, but having him sit here offering to help them sure was a strong case for his innocence.

And that also might be a wrong assumption.

THIRTY-SEVEN

September 26th, 2016
Las Vegas, Nevada

LOTT LOOKED AROUND and then had the very sudden realization that if Paul was who he said he was, and he was telling them the truth, his life and all of their lives right now were in great danger from some seriously deranged people wanting to stop him.

They needed to have their guard completely up before something else went sideways on them. They needed to be in control.

"Everyone down and away from the windows," Lott said.

He couldn't believe he hadn't thought of this before now. They had just been standing and sitting there, open targets.

It didn't take Andor, Julia, and the chief a fraction of a second to act. He moved over as well with his back to a wall and out of any target sight from outside.

All of them had guns drawn and were against walls beside windows, leaving only Paul sitting out in the open looking suddenly stunned and confused.

"Paul, would you please crawl under that table right there and stay out of sight completely."

Paul dove for the table and disappeared under it.

Lott grabbed his phone and got Mike.

"How long until you can have a full protection detail around my house, sniper guards and all?"

"Twenty minutes to scan the neighborhood to make it all clear, another twenty to secure it completely," Mike said without even asking why.

"Please hurry," Lott said. "And get a detail around Fleet and Annie and Doc as well at their offices. I'll warn them you are coming."

"That bad?" Mike asked.

"Could be some very desperate people wanting to cover up a lot of killings," Lott said. "We have Paul Walter, aka Paul Vaughan, in the house here willing to help."

"Jesus, good thinking," Mike said and hung up.

Lott, without looking at anyone else at their posts beside the windows, called Annie.

"We have Paul Walter here in the house and he's basically turning against The Families, as he calls them. I have Mike's people on the way to set up a protection detail around this house and your offices. Stay put until they get in place and stay away from windows."

"Will do," Annie said without a question, understanding the situation perfectly. "I'll call you back when we are secure here."

Lott hung up and glanced at Julia, who nodded to him.

"Great thinking, partner," Andor said.

"Do I need to call in my people?" the chief asked.

Lott pointed at the boards. "Not until we make sure which ones of your people are on the right side of things."

"You know my chief in Reno?" Julia asked.

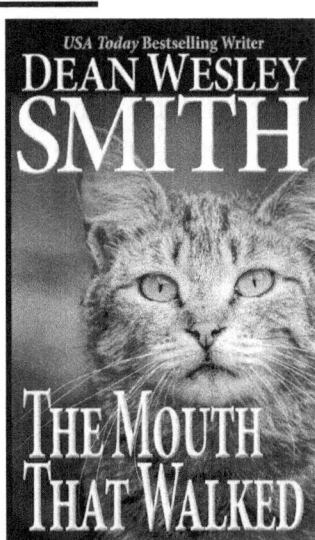

Some Classic Dean Wesley Smith Stories
Available at your favorite booksellers.

The chief nodded.

"Chief Norbert is one of the main family leaders," Paul said from under the table. "Detective Lott is correct, sir. Trust no one until verified. And we can only hope that no one saw me come here. Hopefully, in their arrogance, they would never consider me this stupid, since they have worked hard to pin all this on just me."

The chief looked stunned for a moment, then nodded.

"Dinner will be slightly delayed, however," Andor said.

Lott laughed and the chief actually smiled.

And then they just all waited.

THIRTY-EIGHT

September 26th, 2016
Las Vegas, Nevada

JULIA WAS SURPRISED at how short of a time it was before they were safe, but it felt much, much longer.

It was almost exactly thirty minutes before Mike came walking into the house. Mike nodded to the chief, then turned to Lott.

"All secure, no one around at all. And we have Annie and Doc and Fleet and their people contained and secure as well. And my computer people are standing by to help on the research."

"Perfect," Lott said. "Thank you. Can you hold this for a few hours and give us some time here?"

"We have it for as long as you need us," Mike said.

At that he turned and left and Julia glanced down at where Paul sat under the table and indicated he should get up. He did slowly, clearly showing his age.

At that moment Lott's phone rang. "It's Annie," Lott said and turned to talk with her and set up the research they were about to do and explain what Paul Vaughan/Walter had said so far.

Julia suggested they all go into the kitchen and see how cold that chicken was getting.

They pulled two more chairs up to the kitchen table and Paul sat to one side and to the back against the window where all of them could watch him. Her gut told her he was telling the truth, what he had said so far, but so many things had been false leads on this case before now, she wouldn't trust a word he said about anyone until they could verify it.

After everyone had a piece of the fantastic-smelling chicken, Julia said to Paul, "Do you mind if I open a line to our computer research people to check on some things you tell us?"

"Please," Paul said, wiping his fingers on a napkin. "But tell them to be extra careful. The families have a couple of pretty good computer people."

Lott laughed and said, "Thanks. We have already seen that. But the people working on this for us are far, far better."

"Good," Paul said, nodding.

Julia called Annie and quickly told her what they were doing and that they were planning on asking Paul a lot of questions, so it might be logical that she have an open line and be able to hear the answers directly to do the research and pass on what was needed to Mike and his people as well.

Annie thought that was a good idea, so Julia put her on speaker and set the phone down between her and Paul.

"Can you explain the history of the families one more time to Annie and our computer people," Lott asked Paul.

He did, giving more details than he had the first time about locations in Massachusetts and in Florida.

"We're digging into that," Annie said over the speaker phone.

"Give some to Mike's people as well," Lott said. "They are standing ready."

"Already have them in the loop," Annie said.

Julia was very pleased at how well this machine that Annie and Doc and Fleet had worked. They just shifted into high gear on a moment's notice.

The chief nodded to that as well. Most police districts loved working with Doc and Annie and Fleet because of the fire-power and sophistication they brought to any case.

"So what made the families move to Nevada?" Andor asked.

"One of the burial sites in Florida was found and the pressure was getting too much," Paul said. "They first moved, however, to Los Angeles, where I was born. The families stayed there until the 1970s and then right before my parents were killed moved to Nevada, splitting to both Reno and Las Vegas."

Julia didn't want to ask this next question, but she did. "Have the murders been happening through the entire century?"

Paul nodded. "No one in the family knows about that side of things until they reach twenty-one and are deep in the rest of the beliefs and sexual freedoms."

Julia just sat back.

"We're talking thousands of deaths," the chief said.

"I'm afraid so, sir," Paul said. "The family keeps exact records on every sacrifice, as they call their victims. Since the turn of the century the family has kept pictures and names and details of every sacrifice in their main temple, which is actually nothing more than a compound."

"What kind of compound?" Andor asked.

"Defensible," Paul said. "The families are far from stupid. More than likely they are already planning on vanishing and moving. And if attacked in their compound, they can defend it."

"How much time do you think we have?" Andor asked.

"They have set up elaborate details about me being a mass murderer," Paul said. "I learned this from a few old friends still inside the families, I think, on a ruse to pull me and my wife back inside."

"That was the trail we have been following," Lott said.

Paul nodded. "Which is why I am sitting here now," he said. "But once they realize their ruse has been broken, they will kill their current sacrifices and vanish to the winds. They have spent many, many thousands of hours on such a plan and constantly upgrade it."

"Does everyone know where they are going?" Julia asked.

Paul shook his head. "Everyone has been given very tight false identities that are updated annually. Instructions are to just go and find another safe place to live and the families will be in contact when a new location is set."

"And the killings would start again at that point," Lott said.

Paul nodded.

"So the only way to stop this cult is to take out all its leaders so they can't start a new place?" Andor said.

"That might work," Paul said. "But it would be better to get all of the active members at once."

Julia just felt sick to her stomach.

THIRTY-NINE

September 26th, 2016
Las Vegas, Nevada

LOTT SAT AT the kitchen table, just thinking. Around him everyone had a half-eaten piece of chicken on their plate and no one, not even Andor, seemed to be wanting to eat more.

"Can I ask a question?" Annie said over Julia's phone.

"Please," Paul said.

"Do you think this escape plan would be on a computer somewhere?" Annie asked.

"More than likely yes," Paul said. "Maybe on two. One in the compound in Reno and one in the compound here."

Lott suddenly saw where his daughter was going. If the escape plans and names and such were generated on one or two computers, she and her people could hack them and get that information.

"Can you give us locations of the compounds?" Annie asked.

"I've never been to either," Paul said, "but both properties would have been secured under my great-grandmother's maiden name of Westerfield. Gloria Westerfield. Both would be acreages outside of both towns. But careful on the searches."

"We're careful," Annie said.

Lott glanced at Paul. "Got any idea how many main members there are of the families, ones participating in the rituals and beliefs?"

"Over thirty," Paul said, shrugging, "not counting spouses."

"We're going to need half an army to go in after that many people at the same time," the chief said.

Lott agreed to that.

"Paul, can you help us with the names on the boards, so we can start clearing detectives to help in this?"

"Glad to," Paul said. "The sooner this is over, the sooner my wife and I can live our first day together not in fear for our lives."

Lott could understand that. If you were born into a family that worshipped killing and thought life was cheap, that would be a logical fear.

They headed back into the dining room with Julia carrying the phone and Annie still on the line. Lott decided there were things he needed to clear up sooner rather than later.

"So let's start back quickly with how we got into this. Becky Penn and the other three women under her body in that desert grave. And why did you stage a suicide and who actually died?"

"I had nothing to do with anything around those women's deaths," Paul said. "In fact, when those bodies were first uncovered and Becky was identified, my wife and I realized that the families had been setting me up for years and had kept that as a piece of insurance. Of course, I never would have lived long enough to go to trial. And even if accused, who would believe a serial killer's word about a strange cult full of reputable people."

Lott nodded to that.

"So what about the suicide?"

"I didn't know about it until after it had happened," Paul said. "I was already

Now Available
from all your favorite booksellers in trade paper and electronic editions.

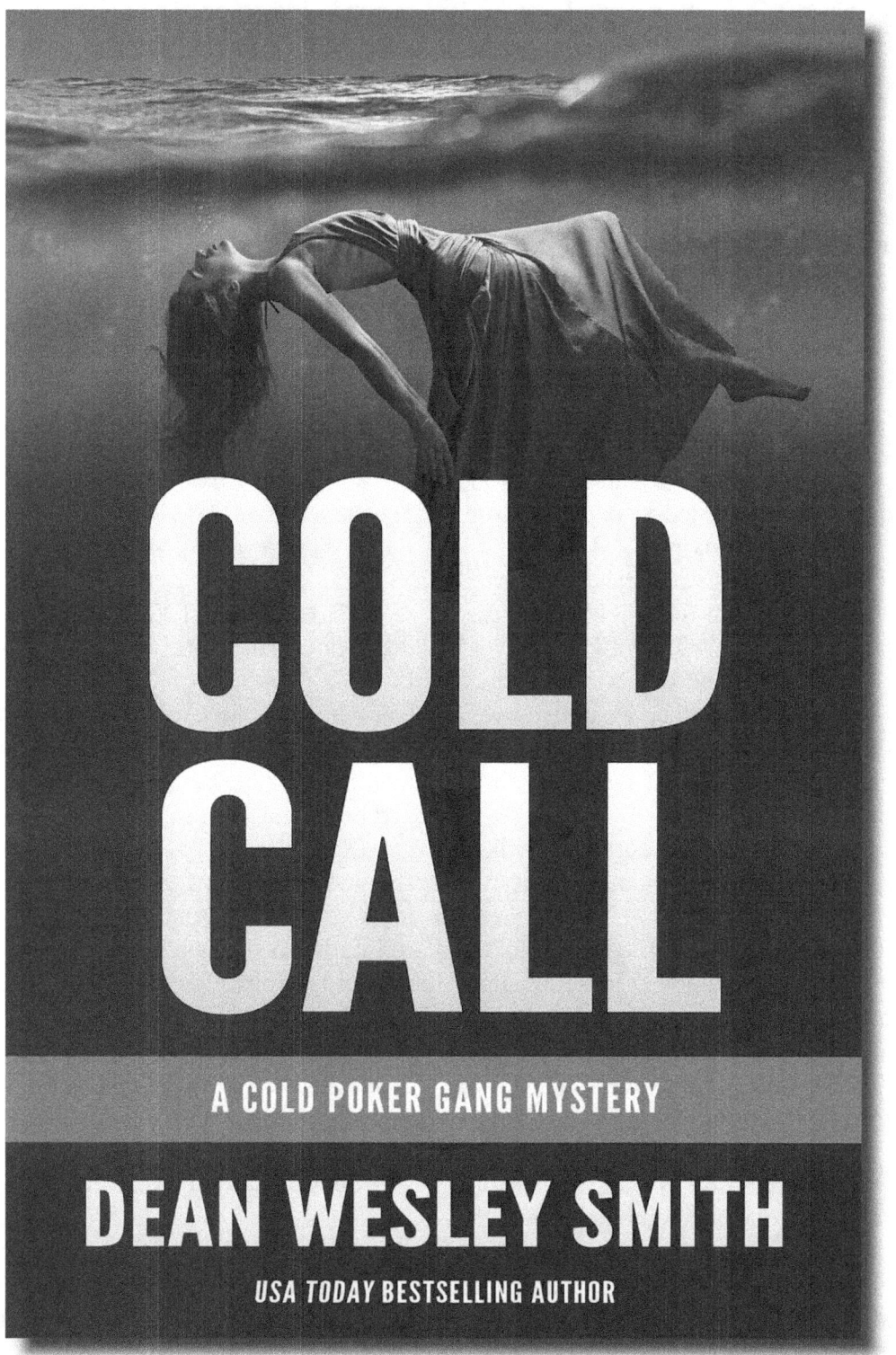

COLD CALL

A COLD POKER GANG MYSTERY

DEAN WESLEY SMITH

USA TODAY BESTSELLING AUTHOR

married to my wife and living under the Walter name. I have no idea why they did that or who that poor soul was who died."

"And the person who pretended to be your sister?"

Paul shrugged. "One of the family members. Again, my wife and I knew nothing about anything."

"That finally makes sense out of that fake diary," Andor said. "And your sister just happening to find it all these years later. But got any idea why the families decided to turn it in and expose those murders?"

"Cleaning up," Paul said. "It is very important to the families to bury all their sacrifices in a sanctioned graveyard on family property. That had happened back in the fight with me to pull me into the families and it needed to be cleaned up. Typical family thinking."

"And you never sold cars to Maxwell or bought the land outside of town used as a burial ground?" Julia asked.

"I haven't talked with Maxwell since my first wife died. When we turned twenty-one, he went full into the families and their beliefs and I went the other direction."

Andor nodded and Lott could tell he was satisfied. Finally, some of this was starting to make sense.

After that, they turned back to the boards and started another board of names that were all major family members in the two cities.

And twenty minutes later Annie broke into the conversation.

"We got in," she said.

"In where?" Lott asked before anyone else could. Julia had put the phone on the table so Annie could hear all the discussions and send the names on to her people and Mike's people.

"We found both compounds," Annie said. "We hacked into both compound's computers and have all their plans of escape and all the fake names of every member and so on. They might run, but none of them will be able to hide when we kick this anthill over."

"Fantastic!" Lott said and everyone cheered.

Lott glanced at Paul. He had dropped into a chair and it looked like he might actually start crying, the relief was so intense.

A lifetime of relief.

FORTY

September 26th, 2016
Las Vegas, Nevada

JULIA FELT EXHAUSTED after three hours of working with everyone to clear names, to make sure the chief had detectives he could trust, and so on. Actually, there were only two family members in the Las Vegas police force and both were beat cops.

They had no overall plan yet, and she was starting to feel like there needed to be one. It was Annie who started that rolling when she came on over the phone and said simply, "We have all the victims' records as well."

"What?" Lott asked, glancing back at the phone on the table where it had sat with an open line for three hours on speaker phone. At one point Julia had run an extension cord to it to keep it powered up.

"Our hacks into the two compounds have retrieved every victim the family has killed since their days in Florida,"

Annie said, her voice soft. "It's a lot of people, more than I can grasp."

"Oh, god," Paul said, his head down and his hands covering his face. "I was born in a family of monsters."

Julia didn't argue at all with that.

"Do I want to know how many?" the chief asked.

"No sir, you don't," Annie said. "But these family members are so egotistical after not getting caught for so long, they kept perfect records of everything."

"What kind of records?" Julia asked.

"Records that show every detail of which family member took part in the kidnapping, which took part in the sex with the victims and when, who was in the room for the final beating rituals, who delivered the final, death blow, and who had sex with the victim in the first few hours after death."

Silence filled the dining room.

Julia just wanted to be sick.

Annie went on. "They kept records of it all as a form of status and advancement in the families. The more you did, the more you advanced into the good graces of their god they called the great one. As far as we can tell, every living member older than 21 years of age in the Reno and Las Vegas area took part in the kidnappings and killings in one way or another except for Paul, his wife, and two other couples."

Julia glanced at Paul who still sat with his head down, then she looked up at the board. The names underlined who lived in Vegas and Reno seemed to fill the boards.

"How many total?" Lott asked, his voice softer than Julia had heard in a long time.

"Sixty-seven," Annie said. "Some are couples, but we have all their names and addresses and so on. And the locations of the other three graveyards for this area, two graveyards for the Los Angeles area, and the graveyards in Florida that were not found."

Julia looked at the chief and he just shook his head.

"We're going to need to get all this evidence with real search warrants," Andor said.

The chief nodded. "Critical. Or these sickos walk free."

"These people are very, very egotistical," Annie said. "They have backups of the family records in the cloud and on hard drives in safe deposit boxes, as well as on the computers in the compounds. I think Paul's statements will be more than enough to get the warrants to make all this information legal when you get to it."

Paul looked up and said, "I'll help any way I can. Dear god, please let me help."

Julia could tell he had been crying. She couldn't imagine what he was going through. His first wife murdered, his fiancé killed by them as well, and he and his wife living every day in fear of death. Now all that seemed to be near an end.

Seemed.

Julia wanted to make no assumptions yet.

"Chief," Lott said, "what can we do to help?"

The chief nodded, knowing Lott was passing the entire mess over to him at that moment.

The chief took a deep breath. Up until that moment he had just been another older detective like the rest of them. But with that deep breath, he stepped back into the strong Chief of Police Julia knew and liked.

The chief turned to Paul. "I need you to stay here and sign some documents in an hour or so. I need to get this in front of a judge by midnight."

"Moving tonight on all this?" Lott asked.

Julia seemed surprised as well. It was almost ten in the evening.

"I sure see no choice," the chief said. "We don't dare hold a day and take a chance on any of this leaking to them."

The chief turned to the phone on the table. "Annie, can you deliver to me in my office ten sets of all these data for both Reno and Las Vegas. Everything since the families moved here, and all the addresses and such of each family member involved. And have Mike and Heather and Doc and Fleet join me there with you. I need Heather's and Doc's connections to the FBI in San Francisco and Reno to round them up there."

"We'll all be there in one hour," Annie said.

Lott spoke up. "Annie, make sure Mike keeps the guards up on this house. Paul is going to be here with us."

"Will do, Dad," Annie said.

"I assume the raid is going to happen on the Las Vegas compound tonight?" Paul asked, standing to face the chief. "May I be there, under arrest or guard, I don't care. I just want to see this end with my own eyes."

Julia nodded. "Sir, we would like to be there as well. Not on the front-line, but seeing this end, since we dug up this mess."

The chief laughed. "On two conditions. First, you keep him alive."

He pointed to Paul.

"Second, you stay out of the press and next time you invite me for chicken, make sure it's not to talk about a mass murder."

"Deal," Lott said.

FORTY-ONE

September 27th, 2016
Las Vegas, Nevada

LOTT HADN'T BEEN this tired in a long time. It was almost three in the morning. He hadn't stayed up until this hour for a very, very long time. And it had been a very long day as well. But at the same time, excitement was coursing through him.

He had had far too much caffeine and he felt slightly jittery.

The streets of Las Vegas still had traffic, but it mostly seemed like support trucks and vans. Very few tourists were out and about and all the lights of the entire city still lit up the night sky as they did all night long.

The compound for the families was located on a hill to the north of town in a very nice area of homes.

He and Julia sat in the front seat of his Cadillac and Andor and Paul sat in the back seat. They were two blocks down the road from a large, gated complex of buildings that looked like regular two-story suburban homes.

The night air was still warm, but not the blistering heat of earlier in the day. It actually felt comfortable and had a light smell of sagebrush.

Julia had her phone on her lap open to Annie.

Annie was also nearby in another car with Doc and Mike and Heather. Lott knew a dozen squad cars were standing by farther down the hill behind them.

From the outside, the family compound looked like a gated subdivision, but all the buildings inside were owned by one person, and two dozen family members lived in the homes inside the complex.

Nice homes from what Lott could tell. The family clearly took care of its own.

Mike, in the meeting with the chief of police, had suggested that he have his people go in ahead of the detectives. His people, as he called them, were Special Forces. They were trained to deal with compounds like this one. They could go in and take out any guards and shut down alarms before the police went through the door. And never fire a shot.

Annie told them later that after the police and a couple of trusted top detectives looked at the compound layout for Las Vegas, the chief had agreed. He had no desire to lose men in a firefight with killers who had nothing to lose.

Mike said he could get ten Special Forces men ready to breach in two hours. Five of them were already ready to go and had been guarding Lott's home and five more had been around Annie and Doc's office.

In Reno, the FBI was working with Special Forces as well, since they could trust no one in the local police department. In fact, one of the people they would be arresting tonight was the chief of police in Reno.

Mike's men had gone in ten minutes ago, scaling the compound walls in four places. There had been no alarms sounded and no shots fired so far.

Now everyone was just waiting for the all clear.

Lott had the window on his side down slightly to listen for any kind of sounds of gunshots. The police were going in at the first sound of a gunshot. But Mike had promised no gunfire. And as well as Lott knew Mike, he had a hunch there wouldn't be any.

The minutes stretched onward.

Lott couldn't believe their one cold case had turned into such a military-style invasion. And that Becky Penn was just the tip of a massive cult of killings.

And if they were lucky, it would end tonight.

But first they had to get through this night to make sure it really ended.

No word from either Reno or the compound in front of them.

And there was to be no other movement to arrest any of the other family members who lived around town until the compounds were secure or in a fight.

Lott had been impressed at how many men the chief had gotten at three in the morning. There had to be forty detectives backed up with dozens and dozens of patrol cops all scattered over town. The idea was that every family member killer around town would be rounded up in a ten-minute span once the word was given to go.

As they sat there, Lott also knew that cells in the jail were being cleared of vagrants and DUI cases and other small crimes to make room for entire families of serial killers.

At eighteen minutes after Mike's men went in, up by the main gate of the compound, Lott could see a man in all black with his gun slung over his shoulder, push open the gates.

"It's clear," Annie said over the speaker-phone in Julia's lap. "All police are moving in on the other family members."

Lott sat and waited until the police had swarmed the front gate and gone in, then he moved them up and parked behind the mass of blinking police lights.

The four of them got out and Lott turned to Paul. "Stay with us."

Paul nodded, looking completely stunned at what was going on.

The chief was standing just inside the compound gate as the first handcuffed prisoners were led out of the closest house.

"Did you read them their rights?" the chief asked the two detectives.

"Read and understood," one detective said as they headed for a car.

Lott studied the compound. Standing on the street like this it looked like a typical cul-de-sac in any subdivision. Ten modern houses, with the biggest at the end.

But this street and these houses were the ultimate modern horror.

"So how did it go?" Lott asked the chief as Annie and Doc joined them.

Doc stood taller than Lott and was in top shape. He had dark short hair and tonight was wearing jeans and a polo shirt and tennis shoes. He and Annie just fit perfectly together.

"Mike's people had them all in zipties before they gave the all clear," the chief said, shaking his head and smiling.

"So where did Mike's people go?" Annie asked, looking around.

"And where did Mike and Heather go?" Lott asked. "Wasn't he with you?"

"He's headed back to keep the pressure on the research," Doc said. "Not the kind to hang around."

"And Mary May? And the guy kidnapped at the same time?" Julia asked.

"Alive and in the basement of that house there," the chief said, pointing to the second house up the street. "That was their ritual house. We have ambulances coming for both of them. The two are in tough shape but will survive, thanks to all of you."

Lott felt like a ton of weight lifted suddenly from his shoulders. He made

himself take a deep breath of the warm night air just to try to slow his fast-beating heart.

They had given closure to a lot of cold cases, but they had also saved lives.

And who knows how many lives off into the future.

Julia took his hand and squeezed it. He glanced at her and could see she felt the same way by the huge smile on her face.

FORTY-TWO

September 27th, 2016
Las Vegas, Nevada

JULIA WAS SO excited that they had saved the kidnapped victims.

The chief went to supervise the arrests and Julia and Lott and Annie and Doc and Andor and Paul moved to one side of the street on the sidewalk and stood in a small line like watching a parade.

Only there was no cheering and this parade was of serial killers.

They all just stood silently watching as family member after family member was led to a police car.

And they watched as Mary May and the other victim were taken from a house on a stretcher and sped away in two ambulances.

The police just kept bringing out more family members after that. Usually two and three at a time, each escorted by a detective and a uniformed cop.

The family members looked so normal, so regular, especially in their bathrobes and pajamas coming out of their modern homes. Yet Julia knew that she was watching one of the worst parades of killers ever to be arrested. How could such normal people living such seemingly normal lives be so evil?

Paul just stood between Andor and Lott, shaking his head as family member after family member walked past. Some of them were sobbing, some of them saw him standing with the police and shook their heads.

Paul and his wife were going to need to disappear under other names after these trials were over. In most places he would be considered a hero for helping to bring down so many murderers. But some family members of victims might wonder why he didn't do this before their daughter or son was killed.

Julia knew. But that explanation would not hold for many. And she understood that as well. So Paul's best hope was to stay out of the press and then vanish into protective custody when this was over. Maybe even tonight if the chief was thinking.

A few times a couple women and men from social services came up the sidewalk and then escorted young children down the street to waiting cars. Julia felt bad for those children. They just lost their parents and were soon to find out they were being raised by monsters.

Finally, Julia saw Lorraine and Ray Walter being led down the front sidewalk from their big house at the end of the block. Both were wearing robes and slippers and Lorraine had a hairnet of some sort over her hair.

The chief of police walked close behind them.

Lott and Julia and Paul stepped forward.

Ray saw Paul and shook his head. "I knew we should have killed you with your parents and sister."

"Ray!" Lorraine said sharply. "Keep your damn mouth shut."

Julia saw the police chief smile and then shake his head. Lorraine and Ray had been read their rights, so what idiot Ray had just said would be admissible in court if any of this ever got that far.

"And why we let you marry our daughter is beyond me," Ray said, spitting at Paul's feet. "Should have killed both of you and put you with your first wife and that other woman you were going to marry."

"Ray," Lorraine said, again as sharp as Julia ever imagined the woman could talk.

The chief was damn near laughing out loud behind them now. The two detectives who were escorting the two just shook their heads and smiled as well.

"Nice seeing you one last time, Lorraine and Ray," Julia said. "Thanks for all the help solving this case."

Ray looked like he might just explode his face was so red.

Julia and Lott just smiled.

"It was her stupid idea to even talk with you," Ray said, almost backhanding Lorraine, and he might have if not in handcuffs and in the grasp of a detective.

And then Ray looked at Paul. "And her idea to keep you alive as well."

"Why did you kill my family?" Paul asked, his voice low and seemingly calm.

"Because with you and your damn sister coming along," Ray said, sneering, "your stupid father was going to continue to control the families and he wasn't smart enough to deserve to do that."

Lorraine just shook her head and looked at the street.

Paul indicated all the police cars around them. "Seems you weren't so good at it yourself."

Ray tried to lunge at Paul, but the detective yanked him back into place so hard, Julia was sure it might have broken some old bone.

"Goodbye, Ray," Paul said. "May the great one, or whatever sick god you bow to, show no mercy on your stupid head."

With that, the two detectives led them on down the street.

The chief smiled at the three of them.

"From what I have been told," he said, "Every active family member in town and in Reno has been caught and arrested."

"Oh, thank you," Paul said, trembling.

"You're going to need to come with me," the chief said to Paul. "We'll get you set up in a safe hotel and you can have your wife return when you feel safe. But we need you giving as much testimony on this as you can over the next week or so."

"My wife can help with that as well," Paul said. "We both want to."

Paul turned to Julia and Lott and Annie and Andor and Doc. "Thank you all for allowing me the chance to explain and doing the work to back up my story. My wife and I owe you our lives."

Julia nodded and Lott shook his hand. "Good luck."

With that, Paul and the chief headed down the sidewalk.

Julia had no doubt they would ever see Paul again. He would vanish into the system for his own protection. And maybe be able to live a life free of the idea he might be killed at any moment.

Then steps down the street the chief looked back at them and smiled. "Remember your promise about the press. You had better get out of here."

Lott glanced at Annie and Doc and Andor. "Bellagio Café?"

"Where else at this hour of the morning?" Andor asked.

"Where else at any time of the day?" Annie asked as they all headed out the front gate and to their cars.

Julia felt lighter with every step.

FORTY-THREE

October 5th, 2016
Las Vegas, Nevada

IT HAD BEEN well over a week since every member of the families was arrested. Lott had been surprised that not a one managed to escape and not a shot was fired considering how fast the entire thing had come together.

There had been no mention of the Cold Poker Gang or Mike and his people or Doc and Annie or Paul in the massive press storm that had hit the national news. The chief and other agencies were keeping them all out of it. And the press storm showed no signs of easing because of the nature of three states being involved.

And the FBI was totally and officially involved now, which helped a lot.

Florida had just started to dig one of the family graveyards, California would be starting over the next few days, and both Reno and Las Vegas had started to get ready to bring up the bodies.

The lists of the victims was still a secret and if a family asked, then their child would be either confirmed or denied as being part of the killings. At the moment it was the best the police could do.

Two family members had attempted suicide and both had failed. Lott liked that. They hadn't given all their victims an easy way out, no reason they should have one either.

And the underage children of the families had all been taken out of state and split up. No telling what would happen to any of them. They were victims of their parents' evil as well.

No real details about the ritual killings had come out yet, but Lott was sure that they would, and that would keep the press circling for a very long time, considering that some of this went back to old cults in Massachusetts.

Annie and Doc had headed off to a poker tournament in London.

Fleet had gone back to Boise, and today, Julia was moving in with Lott.

It was ten in the morning when the movers had arrived at Julia's apartment. They had both gotten up early and done the final packing. Lott had put the last of his clothes in his car and a bunch of Julia's precious small things.

The movers did one trip to take furniture to Julia's daughter Jane's apartment, then came back and made another trip of stuff to a charity.

Then the last trip they loaded up all of Julia's clothes and things she wanted to keep and a couple of rocking chairs and a recliner she loved for the living room.

She and Lott had stood and watched the three young men move in a way that Lott could only barely remember ever moving when he was young.

"So you going to miss this place?" Lott asked Julia as they stood to one side in the almost empty living room of the apartment.

She took his hand and squeezed it. "Not in the slightest."

She pointed to three boxes sitting to one side. "See those?"

"Yeah," he said, slightly worried.

"Those are the clothes I couldn't fit in the closet here."

"So you're moving in with me for my closet?" he asked, smiling at her.

She pulled his head closer and kissed him. And that felt wonderful and he didn't want it to end.

Then when she finally let him go, she said, "Yes, of course."

He laughed. "I knew it. Nothing more?"

"The kitchen," she said laughing. "I've got boxes of dishes and pots and pans you know."

"We have room," he said, laughing. "So nothing else at all?"

"Well, she said, giving him a sly look, "maybe the sex."

"Why, young lady," Lott said, laughing, "I am shocked."

"Not as shocked as you are going to be tonight in bed," she said.

She once again pointed to the boxes. "I have some pretty fine lace things tucked away in there that no one has ever seen."

Lott looked around. "Think these guys can move any faster?"

She laughed and kissed him and he knew right then that without a doubt, this was a damn fine day.

~

#1... October 2013

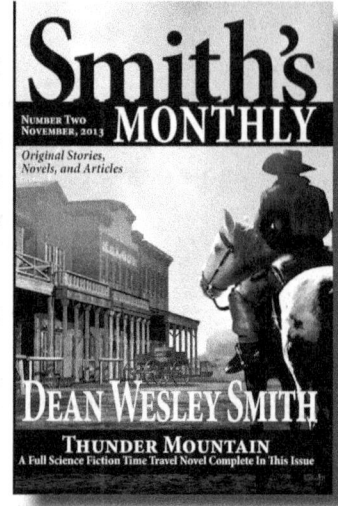

#2... November 2013

#3... December 2013

#4... January 2014

#5... February 2014

#6... March 2014

#7... April 2014

#8... May 2014

#9... June 2014

#10... July 2014

#11... August 2014

#12...September 2014

#13...October 2014

#14...November 2014

#15...December 2014

#16...January 2015

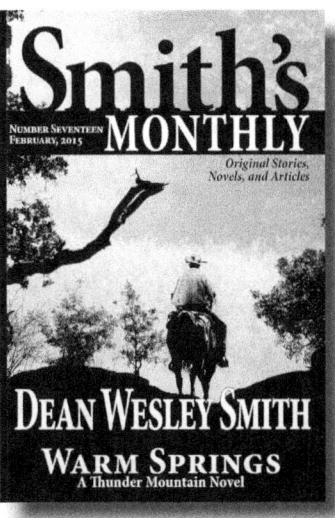

#17...February 2015

#18...March 2015

#19... April 2015

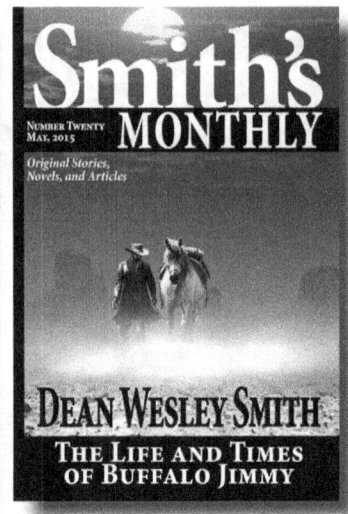

#20... May 2015

#21...June 2015

#22...July 2015

#23...August 2015

#24...September 2015

#25...October 2015

Now Available
from all your favorite booksellers
in trade paper and electronic editions.

USA TODAY BESTSELLING AUTHOR

DEAN WESLEY

SMITH

HEAVEN PAINTED

as a Free Meal

A GHOST OF A CHANCE NOVEL

Thank You!!

I would like to thank the following wonderful people who support my blog and my work through Patreon. Your support is very important to me. Thanks!

Irette Y. Patterson

Chris Cousino

Jane Lawson

Shantnu Tiwari

Rob Cornell

Erick Lindman

Christopher Ridge

Miguel Angel Alonso Pulido

Nancy Hendrickson

Ryan M. Williams

Jacob Proffitt

Marian Goldeen

Brenda Bergeron

John Connelly

Gary Speer

Megan Bryce

Michelle Tatam

Ann Tucker

Kari Wolfe

Terry Mixon

James Husun

Kathryn Rooney

Sherman Cox

Chong Go

Maria Grace

Grondpom

Fen

Livia Quinn

Amri Ackers

Robin Brande

J.R. Murdock

Kathleen McClure

Michael Kelberer

Gunnar Gunderson

F.I. Goldhaber

Mary Jo Rabe

John Kilgallon

Dave Hendrickson